PROTECTRESS

PROTECTRESS

Kendra Preston Leonard

CONTENTS

for my sisters

PRELUDE

Medusa was raped.
Medusa was not raped.
Medusa was given rohypnol.
Medusa lured Poseidon from the sea with a bed of seaweed soaked
      in salt water.
She became pregnant.
She did not become pregnant.
She became pregnant and used her knowledge of the medicinal arts to end
      her pregnancy.
She became pregnant and gave the resulting child to Poseidon to raise.
She gave the child to her own parents, Phorcys and Ceto.
She and her sisters raised the child, who then became a sculptor,
      a psychoanalyst, a designer of prosthetics.
Her body after death produced a winged horse and a golden giant.
Her body after death wept from its palms and the tears mixed with earth to
      create a golem.
Her body after death was dressed by Versace and laid in a bronze tomb
      in Buenos Aires.

Medusa angered Athena.
Athena was jealous.
Athena was not a feminist.
Athena was a prude.
It did not matter to Athena what actually happened to Medusa.

Athena was required to take action by a committee.
Athena was wise but had already had to deal with mansplaining
        gods that night.
Athena was a slut-shaming bitch.
Medusa was made an example of through the great wrath of a
        goddess warrior.

In the long nights, a mortal woman made immortal because of her story ran
from a temple, from a cave, from Kisthene's dreadful plain
seeking blindness, baldness, rebirth
with her sisters.

So many stories. Let us begin anew.

IN THE AGE OF GODS

Phorcys and Ceto were thrice blessed two times:
their first brood was born of the ocean and the land,
part swan, part legend, even at their births.
These Grey Sisters were a trinity
of fashion, of sharing, of making do.
Deino, Enyo, Pemphredo:
like an ancient warhorse, they had but one eye and one tooth.
They saw selectively, ate softly, and walked with a rocking
wave-like gait.

The second weird sister-batch of Phorcys and Ceto
were unequal, but never needed to share.
Stheno and Euryale were born immortal
beneath the gods' mountain.
But the third was born in the light,
and the sun, with its daily rise and fall,
decreed she be mortal.

From the plains of Kisthene
the Grey Sisters watched
their new siblings thrive.
Living by the sea, the second trio
drew salt from the water,
poison from the frogs,

strength from the leaves,
and became healers.

In love with wonder and knowledge
and the appearance of wisdom
and strength,
the sisters gorgon
become enamored of goddesses:
Euryale is drawn to Aphrodite;
Stheno, Artemis;
Medusa, Athena.
Medusa takes vows,
swearing always
to protect the goddess
to serve her
and
to worship her.
Trusting Athena,
Medusa leaves
her sisters and their cave
for Athena's temple.

Mincing no words:
Medusa the beautiful is raped.
As Poseidon pulls away, seal-like,
from between her legs,
or draws back and down,
in his form as a horse,
Stheno, night hunting, finds her sister

in the temple of Athena.
Footprints wet with ocean's foam
and healer's blood grip the marble steps
and point to the departing
form of a man.

Stheno pulls on her helmet
strengthened by the shining scales
of giant fish and
made ferocious with the tusks of a boar
taken by the hunter herself
and stupidly attempts
to attack
a god.

She does not even touch him before
she is thrown by a cutting, hammering wave
onto the white temple floor.

And where Stheno seeks violence
against the god,
the dedicatee of the consecrated ground
takes further unjust action.
Athena curses Medusa,
not caring that she is a victim.

The shame, rages Athena. *The shame you bring.*

As Medusa's hands claw at her head,
a single priest ventures out
of his nighttime hiding hole
to curse the women
further,
as if
that could be done.
And while Stheno crouches to aid her sister,
the youngest of the triplet Phorcydes turns on the man
and makes him stop.

He stops. *He stops.*

All of him stops. His lungs,
his heart, his kidneys stop.
His veins stop. His mouth stops.

And when in anger Stheno throws her helmet at him—
you already know this, of course—he shatters. Priest becomes pebbles,
rubble, dust. Long nights begin.

There is darkness
and cool water.
Euryale bathes her sister,
her eyes,
her bruises,
all over her arms and legs,
and abdomen,
and then each

minute, coiled, delicate, transparent
baby snake.

They emerge from Medusa's scalp
sightless:
they have no eyes themselves.
They seek not to bite or crush
but relish the touch of
the cool skins of one another
and the heat of their—what?
carrier? mother? bearer?—her
head.
Her long locks have fallen away
like the hair Stheno will see
on hospital floors
many centuries from now,
hair lost to other poisons,
poisons that cure.

Late, a different goddess visits,
briefly, as is her wont:
Hecate, who weeps
silently for Medusa and
her serpents.
Her tears add to Medusa's bath,
her soft lamplight embracing the sisters.
I too am three, she says. Although my power
is faint, I offer you blessings:
for healing yourselves and healing others;

for finding your ways home;
for being three;
for bringing light;
for protection;
for Medusa, an immortal life
to protect others.

She stands, fading against the cave walls.
Her voice is low and strong.
You need not sacrifice to me:
I cannot undo what Olympians
have done, but I can light paths
to redress and peace.

Dazed a little by the
goddess's rare appearance,
and still looking to the empty space
from where she has
disappeared into a haze of
glowing air,
Euryale sings a soft song
a lullaby. And then a fiercer one
to help her test her own mettle
and matter
and she looks into
Medusa's eyes
and lives.

And sighs.

Sisters, she says, I think we three
at least are safe. Together. Here.
But Stheno hears the battering sea at their cave door,
riled Poseidon beating with both fists against their hideaway
and Athena, far above, howling at her
former priestess:
shame, shame, shame you should die rather than bear this shame
and she replies no, we are not safe.
Hecate's gifts may armor us,
we may live forever,
and we may be safe from Medusa's eyes,
but we are not safe from these gods.
Would we could not believe in them
that they had no power over us
over any
over the natural world.
They should be so cursed
to be forgotten.

But the gorgons cannot hide
because Medusa cannot
stop
screaming.
She screams in anger and pain
at the goddess to whom she gave her love
her admiration and heart
all for nothing.
Given the rape culture
of the gods,

she is less furious with Poseidon
and more saddened, no—
it is not sadness,
but an emotion she doesn't
know how to name.
A kind of stunned hurt
with swaths of rage,
and a bit
of resignation.
When she thinks of him,
her breath becomes short
and shaky, rippling through
her nose
and her eyes fill
with sea water
that she cannot let fall;
instead,
she lies in the dark,
thinking, incredulously,
He just raped me.
Just is temporal,
just denotes the ease
with which her
attacker surprised
and forced her,
just suggests how much
worse
he could have done.

When she dreams, Medusa
stands on a ledge
from which it is all too tempting
and easy to fall. There are no
guards, no rails, no
helping hands.
What god would help her?
Her trusted protector,
grey-eyed Athena, can only see
in black and white.
Medusa's screams and
questions and
hoarse, croaking pleas go
unanswered.

While her sisters
hunt for food and medicine,
trapping tiny frogs,
shooting wild goats,
Medusa cannot leave.
Many hours, she cannot move,
frozen as much as
one of her own
be-gazed-upon
victims.

Her distress—what a dainty word,
far too close to princess or fancy-dress,
so no, not distress—

her sheer terror wraps around her like
wet linen, keeps her immobile,
keeps her from speech,
keeps her fear
embodied.

No prayers, no offerings,
no oxen sacrificed,
no promises made
to Athena assuage the curse.
And as long as those around her
see some kind of justice
in Athena's punishment
of a woman unjustly
treated, there will be no safety
for Medusa.

The gorgons decide
they will leave Greece,
will leave the realm in which these gods,
unjust, unchecked, under water and above the skies,
above punishment, punishing and prowling for mortals to eat,
to suck away life and will as meat from long bones,
can so treat innocents.

But Athena, she of
shame shame you should die rather than bear this shame
makes a different plan, and so
first comes Perseus

and his idiotic mirror
and sword
and sandals:
a stereotype
sent by Athena
through Polydectes
to silence
her screaming
former priestess.

Did you know, asks Stheno,
that his name comes from *perthein*:
to sack, to waste, to ravage?
Euryale snorts. Typical,
she says,
crushing the claws of a wolf
between her fingertips
for a healing plaster,
given that his whole life has
been devoted
to controlling women.

She makes a gesture meaning,
everywhere, just look around you.
His mother, our sisters,
the Hesperides—

He'll use your head as a weapon,
Stheno tells Medusa.

He won't get it, she replies, hoarse-voiced
but resolute.

And so in an all-nighter
to dwarf every all-nighter since,
the sisters put their healing arts
to devious ends.
Stheno makes a mask
of her sister's lovely face,
while Euryale draws forth from the
sea a slithering of serpents
full of toxins.
The Graeae, themselves full of wrath
at the arrogant Perseus for stealing their eye,
make a special sisterly visit,
applying the attributes of their names
to the head:
alarm, horror, dread.
Stheno provides a bodily shape for Perseus to swing at;
Euryale drops the head at his feet.
While it will turn a few unlucky men to stone,
the prouder Perseus becomes of his kill,
the more he displays his gorgon's head,
the more—Euryale snickers—
impotent he will become.

Thus Perseus fooled, three gorgons,
immortal but bruised, angry, and tired,

plan a passage away from the locus
of Medusa's anguish.

The night roads are tricky to the eyes:
Stheno and Euryale lead Medusa
stumbling
over horse trails and divoted paths
low hills with rocky trails and mountains with sharp-
branched trees and brambles.
At times, they take a risk
and take off her eye-wraps.
In three days, though, she has
accidentally created statues of
birds, insects, and nearly an entire herd of sheep
and so she willingly b(l)inds herself again.

Behind the linen strips, she sees
polychrome explosions and circles
and tiny dotted lines and fractions of shapes.
Black and rose gold streamers and yellows
that mankind will not invent in the material
world for millennia
shoot across her closed lids.

Each dusk they leave whatever bolthole they have found—
cave, disarrayed orchard, abandoned hut—and walk, mostly silently,
always away from Greece.
Some nights they move through fog, or clouds, and
no one can see any better than the blindfolded Medusa.

Nights may last minutes or days; time folds and stretches,
the skies shifting above as they walk.

In time, they come to roads rutted from wheels
and paved with flat, gravel-tossed, dun-colored stones.
Roads bring other travelers, men and women and goats,
and places to rest out of the rain and places to eat
things Stheno has not killed for them.

How are you even alive? yells Athena,
Perseus! What has happened?
Shame shame shame...
and the gorgons hurry on.

One morning the world they wake to
is one of wheat and barley and goats
and pigs and dogs and cattle and mud houses
and pottery painted with precise geometry
in red and brown. In the megaron, the people
meet and wed and recite and feast surrounded
by painted walls.

This is civilized! says Stheno.
Let's stay a while.

But the pottery and painted walls doom the idea:
Euryale finds images of her sister, Medusa's face
distorted, her mouth full of too many teeth,

her cheeks bulging and eyes staring,
her snakes hanging like sticks from her head.

The sisters remain too well known,
and their story spreads,
creeping from mouth to ear and back around
again: be wary of three women
traveling together,
two protecting a third, whose face
is wrapped to protect from a plague.
They know not what this plague is:
a curse, an infection,
an imbalance of humors—
but give them no quarter,
these three. Push them away
from cart and barrel and house and barn.
Exhaustion smothers them,
a heavy gauze that binds their arms
to one-night beds of moss and stone and
makes their heads
sickening weights on fragile spines.
They need more time, the sisters gorgon;
much more time of sleep and rest,
so that they might become unknown.
So that they might wake in a different time,
a time when no one draws Medusa's head
on doors or floors or roofs
to keep away evil spirits; a time when no one
believes that Athena's curse was just.

Athena sees them in the city; her hands shake in fury.
You are supposed to be dead! How do you live with the shame?
Medusa winces at the pain in her head.

Avoiding cities now, they find warmth with
a bear, its fur blue-tinged and soft,
sleeping in its cave and apparently happy
—or perhaps just unaware—
that immortals join its slumber.
Cocooned and warm,
three women and a bear
like a tumbled heap of puppies.
They sleep hidden from all gods.

When they wake,
slowly, by turns and small stretches,
the world has changed itself
into something different:
not new—
never new—
but new enough.

The written language is familiar,
but the sounds have changed:
vowels disappear, become one,
all i, i, i.
Consonants are slushed and slow
the crack of ice replaced with the sounds

of old snow gently breaking apart
and melting
under the warm feet
of dogs and children.

Sleeping and protected,
Medusa has built up resistance
to the *shame shame shame*
that still roils Athena
when the goddess sees the gorgon.

STHENO IN SUBURBIA

Stheno's necklace bears a single snake on a staff,
nodding to Asklepios and the gorgons'
Medusa-mothered mascots.

They are mascots, now, the serpents:
Duse, in her comfortable college life,
covers them with chic turbans,
covers her eyes with minutely thin plastic lenses,
and becomes
an oddity, perhaps?
For to many, she is no longer
dangerous,
although thinking her not so
does not make her so in truth.
Students leave her gifts in the forms of
asps and adders, black mambas and boas;
they fill her office,
cuddly soft simulacra of the very real
and sometimes itchy
sightless hatchlings above and around
from her brow to base of her skull.

Stheno comes home
when the sun is pinking the air

around her little house,
its porch raised on short square columns of bricks;
underneath, a hideaway for possums.

She holds a paper bag
against her hip like a child,
closing the car door softly.

She's stopped at the fisherman's stand
on her way home
from the hospital
another night shift—her favorite kind of day—
tucked away into her memory.

Up two concrete stairs, three;
a brindled cat waits,
impatient,
wanting the morning's
catch, leaning and shifting
against Stheno's legs
like the palm trees in the yard.

Cat cat, she says, *gati gati*,
unlocking the door.
They go to the spice-bright kitchen,
where Stheno broils the fish,
makes rice,
and serves them both.

Stheno reads, the morning light
warm and promising wet,
and gati is slipping in and around
Stheno's legs, a furred serpent.
Outside, Miami is still waking,
one sleepy child,
one sleepy woman
at a time;
one ecstatic dog
whom Stheno loves
from a distance,
thinking of Hecate's familiars,
greeting the day with
uncontrollable glee
at being alive for another walk.

The cat watches
from Stheno's bed.
Stheno bathes and oils her long curly hair,
braids it back, slips into the
tight wrap of
purples and lavenders
of the bed. *Gati gati*, she says,
her fingers playing along its back,
go out hunting and then it's time:
gati's out the door
to hunt crepuscular
creatures in the early hour.

Stheno likes to imagine
that she hunts with the cat.
Somewhere inside
where her hunting instincts
have been quieted, she wants
to release them:
to run in the Everglades, skimming the water,
stepping on turtle's backs to spear
meaty alligators, lazing crocodiles.
A. *mississippiensis* has no defenses against
a gorgon on the hunt.
In the Catholic church, she recalls,
alligators are eaten
on Fridays
as
fish.

Stheno dreams as the day rises:
of past sleep,
of the bear, safe and blue,
of days when she and her sisters slept
in a heap, triskelied together,
warm, safe, protective and protected.

Outside, the neighbor Chihuahua
is an alarm clock:
it's eight, he says, get up,
get up, it's eight and
where is my breakfast.

Confined to his yard
and a doghouse,
he can't hunt like gati, claws sharp and lean,
and so when his stomach finds itself empty,
it tells his mouth to let everyone know:
It's eight
and I need breakfast.

Stheno turns in her sleep.
At the hospital, nurses lean over
her patients, checking the snakes of IV lines.
The day nurses are harder and brighter
on the surface than Stheno,
who in the night takes on the
gentled visage of the moon,
soft and glowing pale
in the dark rooms.
Her pastel scrubs and
healing hands silence lights and alarms,
drawing in clouds of the finest,
most sea-treated air to soothe dry hands
and eyes and membranes.

In the morning, children, ill,
miss Stheno, even if they slept through her visits,
their dreams calmed,
their feet encased in fresh socks.
They remember a breeze
that neither burned dry and hot

nor left them clammy and damp.
Old women who have watched
the whole night
also miss Stheno,
who is strong enough to lift them
and kind enough to bring
small bites of foods they loved in their youths.

Stheno measures and pours
she counts and splits and crumbles
she mixes and makes doses
to drink or to inject. She takes
temperatures, pulses, samples, notes.
She jokes and listens and reads
and hears and cleans.
She looks for futures,
sees celebration and death,
two impostors, just the same.

She drinks coffee midway through her shift:
as dark as night,
as sweet as sin,
as strong as love,
or however it has been made,
often indifferently or in a rush,
and sits in its pot.

Stheno dreams:
she dreams of the palm trees

shaking fists to the skies,
dancing salaciously with the wind,
swaying like a drowsy dog.

In any week, Stheno encounters neighbors,
pleasant but distant,
as she prefers.
She's had close neighbors
early on, in an earlier America,
where she was an immigrant
among other immigrants. She remembers
trading bread and eggs and herbal tisanes
and her dresses covered in aprons
and her hands in flour and dust in her hair,
and she remembers a woman named Cass
and her daughter and son and a boarding house
where they all lived for a time. She remembers
Cass's face, where a mole sat by her right ear,
and her son's raw feet at the end of a docks day
and her daughter's wedding.

She remembers the 1940s in Canada, desperate
years and telegrams and trying to gather her sisters
close to her in a place that felt safe
and remained orderly and calm,
her brown house with the irises.

Sometimes Stheno
thinks they should have joined up, the sisters, become

hunters and warriors again, given their might
to the war effort.
But she was frightened, and Euryale too,
in ways they hadn't been in earlier lives.
Stheno felt fragile, somehow: would the new
rotors and screws and rolling treads
destroy bone of even immortals? Medusa
fought and infiltrated her way across Europe
to North America,
sabotaging veins and arteries,
bringing to dust grandiloquent
men,
boys,
women,
girls,
others,
quailing or nasty,
proud or fearful,
any who fattened the camps
and themselves
by feeding their neighbors
to grinding machinery.

When she arrived, mad on the slip,
Stheno and Euryale were there to
collect her; to collect
her rage into casks for later use,
to collect her body into a
blanket, soft and old, to

collect her, as if a package
of near-psychopathy and anger
and renewed desire for creating terror
could be bottled, boxed, enveloped
soothed or cooled from its
magma-like stone boiling point.

Her sisters took Medusa into the forest.
They were not in Stheno's suburbia,
but safety outweighs convenience,
particularly when you are an immortal
being and very self-sufficient.

They disappeared together
for a bit then, the sisters gorgon, hunting and trapping,
assisted and sometimes hindered by Stheno's newest
shaggy farm dogs, giant otters who swam the rivers
and slept in snowdrifts.
They listened, mostly: to stories about the Tseax Cone
and the Ring of Fire; to Nisga'a Wolf women and men;
to the radio, tinny, with voices from an underwater
dream of Britain; to snow breaking branches in the night.
Stheno and Euryale were coated with blubber that winter;
having no hair to rub it into, Duse fed her portions to the snakes.

After the war, Euryale took Duse to France
to be useful there—
she will not say just how, but let us assume
that eyes and stone and sledgehammers

were part of it all—
and
Stheno
returned to hospitals, first in prairie towns
in the north,
then slowing moving southwards,
seeking the sea. She may hate its god,
but she is in essence of the sea herself.

And so after much time in the Midwest
to Miami,
where she ignores the glitter
and sparkle and the beach and the beat
and drinks café Cubano and thick mango
and tastes salt from work and salt from lovers
and sleeps through the sun's path,
waking at twilight,
a benevolent monster with a fishtail braid
and infusing the sick with infinitely small
grains of her own life.

Stheno dreams:
she dreams of the cave, where her sisters
stare at her
trying to impart some message.

She shakes away the dream,
looks at the clock: a bad time to call Euryale,
and Duse is probably out

teaching, or revenging. Stheno knows
her sister still hunts,
albeit selectively and carefully, but
perhaps more now
than ever before: the priestess
turned
vigilante.

Everyone knows
now
the famous
Professor Medusa.
But Medusa's sisters choose to remain
secret.
They use a glamour, perfected
in the cave and made of scales and wings
and special kinds of dust
scraped from stones under
particular moons,
and whiskers of phantom pumas,
the blessings of eels,
and drops of motor oil.
It makes them forgettable,
when they want to be forgotten.

The clock says three
and Stheno thinks sleepily:
the world revolves
around threes,

but not three sisters gorgon,
or even three weirder sisters,
or tender-hearted tripartite Hecate,
and not just in religion,
but in the everyday:
three when school lets out, and
three colors on the stoplight. A
three dog night to keep you warm;
a love triangle can be dangerous,
or a happy polyamorous group.
It is the atomic number
for lithium; human eyes have
three cones. Field goals are worth
three points; now there are
three-point shots. Stheno likes
baseball and hockey:
three strikes, three forwards, hat tricks.

Stheno has lived in America for a very long time,
and many times.
She has lived in cul-de-sacs where the children painted
bases around the circle for kickball,
in towns where she couldn't save teenage boys
from their own weaponized bodies.
She has lived in pristine trailers, parked
perfectly square in a row with others.
She has lived in apartments and
boarding houses, in an attic and a basement.

In Miami, Stheno has learned Haitian Creole, Spanish in three flavors,
how to administer the latest drugs for overdoses, to be knowledgeable
about Cuban politics.
She owns her little house and a set of
hand-painted plates.

For a while, far away from Florida,
she tried an experiment. She lived
with a man, also from the hospital.
He knew she was something primeval
or odd, not of his time,
but she never spoke of it;
and one day he brought home a dog
and talked of how he would likely outlive
this puppy, stroking its feet,
but he could still give it a good life.
And he looked at her and waited.

The dog slept on their bed
and they did not approach the topic
again even once,
but spent many happy weekends
at the dog park, their dog catching a ball
thrown by an immortal woman
wearing jeans and a baseball cap.

After the dog died, after the man died—
not long after and much earlier than they
had expected—

Stheno returned to the cave
by herself for the first time: the sisters
returned together to it every few decades,
drawn by shared dreams calling them there,
to rest and renew and plan newish lives.
Alone, she
listened to the sea and the fish and the boats
and the songs of the ropes and of the sun on the rocks
and found herself apart from time but also apart
from Euryale and Medusa,
and she felt like she had taken oyster shells
and scraped them over her arms and then slowly,
slowly stalked the salt in the sea.
She didn't plan to sleep but when she woke up,
and the cave was cold and not even the hottest of water warmed
her shoulders and legs,
she thought that perhaps the cave didn't like having only one resident.

Her dream now is not the usual one
that calls the sisters to the cave.
Stheno can't remember another dream like it:
Medusa faces her, eyes wide open and mouth the same
both lined with red far too deep for her olive skin,
her snakes uncovered and unshorn,
short but riotous,
twists come to life,
seeking escape from their host;
with one hand Medusa reaches out
to push away

an unseen terror,
her other hand knuckled
around a spear,
and on her shoulders epaulets of rank,
prepared for a war she does not want.

Stheno is shocked by this nightmare of her sister,
who welcomes battle and regularly stamps out
human men,
the mundane bureaucracy in her thrall. Duse never
shirks from a fight:
she embraces anger and vengeance
like she once did Athena—
Athena? were those her grey eyes
shown in speckled armor
covering Medusa's chest and throat?
Was that the sound of owl wings
honing in on prey that woke Stheno
from her sleep and brought her to be
sitting upright as though snatched
from the sheets?

Athena, woken by people seeking old religion
and new meaning, is shouting at Medusa again,
the same old refrain of *shame shame shame*.
When once it would not have traveled,
the sound of her voice is beginning to
reach the gorgons again.

Afternoon light stretches out through the blinds
and *gati* comes in, cleaning her own face,
pleased and clever and, as though Stheno is still sleeping,
lies beside her.

The light, the outside sounds of motorbikes and rough trucks
and a bicycle bell wake Stheno more—
she can't possibly sleep again now—
and she rises and dresses, cotton cocoons
for her limbs, and is nervous.

Cults are cyclical; they return from mud
and persecution or just and righteous condemnation to
spiral outwards, gaining new followers,
and back in again, shedding all but those who have traveled
to the core. Stheno knows
women who grasped at any woman god they could find
stickering the image and dogma of one
over another
to comply or to seek new comfort.
Athena surely has followers who
have brought her to life,
but a life still shaped by an ancient
often unjust time and place.

She'll wait, Stheno thinks. One dream
is no call, no prophesy, no demand.
She'll sit in her living room,
in her mission-style chair,

like any other woman,
and wait. Surely
Duse will call, or Euryale,
if there's a threat.

Stheno eats peanuts, breaking them
between her front teeth.
Gati rests across her thigh,
her little belly full,
a rounded planet surrounded
by the stars that are her eyes and teeth
and white-tipped tail.

Days pass, six, ten.
Stheno is absorbed with a child
in pediatric oncology
who will survive
traumatized,
become an addict,
recover again,
paint murals and trains,
big box stores,
library walls,
the snake room at the zoo.
Perhaps the dream was singular,
an anomaly,
a shadow on an x-ray that
turns out to be nothing.

And so Stheno is sleeping
when the dream returns,
slightly changed:
Euryale staring directly at her,
flipping lenses like an optician
but the lenses are all reflecting
one of Duse's snakes—
a set of snake portraits—
and Euryale's eyes are rimmed red
and she has weapons strapped to her back
that peer out from behind her shoulders
like burnt wing bones
and Stheno jerks and wakes
and the telephone rings.

Stheno can't make it to answer in time,
but it doesn't matter,
and while the *gati* is out
killing a very particular rat from the
house three behind and two to the left
that has taunted her,
Stheno speaks to her sisters.

No no, says Duse, I'm fine,
just teaching some readings that
pricked at my mind,
nothing more—
but Euryale is more cautions,
as she often is and she has had

a dream more than any of them:
a dream with an owl beak and shining helm
and red-eyed sisters whose sight she cannot
salve,
and she sighs and there is silence
and three sisters slump their shoulders a bit
because these are lives they enjoy but
nonetheless, despite their words,
they sink into spells and begin the process
of closing up houses and suspending
lives, all hoping this will be a short cavetime,
one that doesn't require anonymous movers
and storage units or as has happened before,
completely new beginnings,
although Stheno never minds
when she has to go back to school,
an untraditional student in the most
extreme.

Stheno will miss fish and rice with gati-cat
and gati will miss Stheno's warm back in the afternoons
but gati has other houses and places to sleep and eat
not counting the many pernicious rats
and finches and geckos.

Three sisters in different airports
stand in lines with small backpacks
or cases or bags
carrying with them only

changes of clothes that can last
many years if need be. The path home
is always easy.
They will stand in lines
and file on and off transport
and walk and walk
and meet under a hot sky
that has burned away its clouds,
and they stand in line for food
and they drink and eat
and they rise together in a curved
kind of line
and walk into dusk,
sandals on stone,
sandals on sand,
soles on stone.

Their pasts will inform their futures.

MEDUSA DOMINA

Declining to adhere
to her sisters' claims that they
are healers and should dive
again into
their arts, Medusa calls herself
protectress—
although of what or whom
she does not specify—
on a suitably dark night leaves
into or on the sea
and comes ashore in Nicomedia,
where young Constantine
wrestles lions and uses new gods
to fight the old.

When Medusa sees that statues and mosaics of Athena—
now Minerva—a simpering name—
still claim fruit from the trees,
wine and sweet water,
she cannot contain
the loud and immortally reckless
beating of her heart. It shatters
her own ribs. She forces herself
to devour
any residual fear of the goddess—

for now she cannot be killed
and she believes time has leathered her heart—
and takes on the goddess's
own game.

Athena-Minerva herself is too busy being worshipped
to notice the glamour-hidden gorgon aside from
an occasional *why won't you die?* directed in her
general vicinity.

Medusa taunts Athena-Minerva, though:
makes offerings to
the gods of stone.
She hardens olive trees,
freezes owls in flight.
Dressing herself in a chiton
woven by a Sister of Arachne
of silk and metal and the tendons
of sacrificed birds, she dabbles in war,
selling her sight as a weapon
to the emperor from Naissus.
A city is easier to sack
when its citizens
and slaves
are forever still.

This wily man, full of misdirection,
appeals to the gorgon with his
relentless use of the gods

for his own ends,
which are, for the moment,
good enough for her.
Those whom Diocletian ruined,
Constantine restores.
In this, Medusa believes she sees
the end of Athena.

Wide-ranging across the sea,
Medusa becomes
her own war goddess.
Terrors spread, whispered
cloak to cloak
and shield to shield
speaking of Constantine's
dark-robed sorcerer
who casts but a glance
and turns a regiment of men
into a landslide.

Efficient, Medusa's ally
sends enemies to quarry stone
from her newly-made victims.
For her, he not only looks away,
but positively blinds himself
to her other activities.

She rids his armies of vermin:
rats
and
rapists.

It is she who directs the architects
and laborers,
hauling stone veined with
the blood of the Emperor's
foes
to construct his
bathhouses, celebratory arches,
his arenas, his secret tomb.
Medusa feels sated
when the Emperor dies.
His gods are nebulous, despite
propaganda. They are weak and infantile;
the Greek gods are worn down to translucency:
people begin to believe in natural phenomena
instead of irate bullies on a mythical
mountain.

Medusa travels to the Dalmatian coast,
where she takes up residence in Diocletian's
old palace, already falling into disrepair.
She destroys his Temple of Jupiter,
chases out squatters and dogs.
There she lives by the Sea-Gate.
on the southern side of the palace.

She can watch the sea
or slip away
into or on it
as she likes.

The daughter of sea-gods,
Medusa finds that the slender
minions of her scalp are amphibious
and give to her this gift as well.
She dozes in the water, sleeps in tidal pools,
lazily chases fish.

She swims in and out of the Sea-Gate,
walks the decumanus across the vast
fortress day and night
dipping into temples and sanctuaries
to laugh at the gods
and steal the offerings left to them.

Restless, she takes lovers,
keeping her eyes bound
learning muscles and tendons by touch,
nerves and organs and gristle.
She reclines on the palace's dark sphinxes
back to back
with their immoveable solemnity
as men and women and others

all touch and lap and let hands and tongues snake
in and on and around her,
never looking above her breasts.

Medusa's lovers, servants, followers
swap bodies, change clothes.
The Empire falls, the palace crumbles.
She spends more time in the sea,
though it grows colder
and the sky heavier and darker.
She swims the width of the sea,
the length of an ocean.
In her sojourns on land, she sees movement:
people everywhere in bands small and large,
escaping one thing to embrace another,
escaping one thing to find only more of the same.

Becoming fretful in her solitude, Medusa travels
with the bands of men and women and children,
passing as a young blind woman,
her serpents covered like hair that demands modesty,
carrying knives and a woolen blanket.
She wants to hide, to rest, to plot
what to do next.
Geological chaos obliges her.
On a long peninsular place she finds caves
where she and the small people who travel alongside her

wait for wheat to return,
wait for fogs to clear,
wait for the great veil of dust to drop.

The earth shakes and burns and floods
and Medusa cleans bones out of her cave
and waits.

Famine cannot touch her
nor cold nor drought,
though the grit from the dust
penetrates her eyes
and, exhausted by her travail
and her restored fear,
they weep mud and stones.

Athena, whose vast sacred
temples have been disguised
as churches, whose radiant features
now seem to grace another woman's face,
is full of mirth:
she holds a spear, she resists centaur sensuality,
she is attached to a copper-headed queen.

She may be repackaged
but she still has devotees,
both knowing and ignorant
around the Aegean.
Shame, she says but now she says it gently, *shame*.

Your body is a shame and shames you.
Shame.

and under her breath, in her old persona:
why aren't you dead?

And all alike still
blame women
and men and children and those
of no single or opposing sex
for their own rapes.

GORGONS VÖLKERWANDERUNG

Her sisters, too, sought other lives.

Euryale and Stheno travel together
often,
a metaphorical umbilicus linking them
stretching, contracting.
They try on lives like costumes
knowing that they will always
eventually
become tired or bored or annoyed
and trade in one identity for another.
What doesn't change is their charge
as healers. They seek medical reparation
for Medusa's transforming gaze.

They move from group to group
of the Völkerwanderung,
idly examining and pocketing
languages, foods, garb,
ideas, patterns of living.

They are in York, Tintagel,
Ravenna. They watch at Ongal;
they witness the battle and the peace.
Euryale rides with Khazars

while Stheno goes to the Caliphate.
One to India, one to Denmark.
Each gathers medicines, ointments,
recipes for red eyes, the liver, cold toes;
lenses for their sister.

Euryale grinds stone, minerals, bee's wings
in laboratories she has made. At the end of
long nights and days,
she packs slides of thin hard rock
and sends them to her sister.
After years of
grinding and no reduction
in the small stone animals
on which Medusa tests her glasses,
Euryale throws herself
into new experiments,
singularly putting aside
the problem of stone-making eyes
for a time. Like her sister earlier,
she decides to take on the persona of a god;
she has always worshipped Aphrodite.

In a room of weavings and embroideries,
Euryale holds the breasts of her lovers
one in both hands, each in a hand,
one in both hands, one with her lips.
Cool and smooth, they enflame her
own mouth. Her nipples rise like dragon's heads,

her lips open, grow, need.
She is chivalrous: she maintains orders of
votaries to whom she teaches poetry,
the stars, the opening and apex of the
Roman de la Rose, countless orgasms, salves and balms.

Each gallant adapts her own vows,
playing on the Enterprise of the Dragon's Mouth,
with long strokes of tongue and long, deft fingers,
trying to avoid being burnt.
The Enterprise of the Green Shield and the White Lady,
a game of blindfolds and hiding and slow
generous
striptease.
The Enterprise of the Prisoner's Iron, role-playing
as captives, or enchainment, enchantment, or
student teaching teacher.
Votaries enter her chamber and she theirs without
suspicion or doubt, but playfully, carefully observing the
temperature of the room, or skin, of water
as it climbs and cools.

When Euryale returns to her optical work,
finding a balance between the occupation of her mind
by the hips of her lovers and her familial compulsion
to somehow fix her sister,
she is surrounded by glimmering
light: crystal, glass, precious stone.
Some of these most polished and satiny

objects have found their way to the Prisoner's Iron,
their even, unbroken lengths and roundnesses
moving in fluid and fluid in motion, plumbs for
intimate depths, mere jewels to the uninitiated.
But others here are trained for more clinical
purpose: to shield the eyes of Medusa.

Dark, pink quartz, labial in color, is too clouded
for viewing the world. Eroticism has its place
in the everyday,
but Medusa must see clearly
when she chooses.

There are too many clouds.
Euryale works in refinement,
refining touch, perception,
a single nail
across the spine, a single lens
across the eyes.

Returning to Ptolemy, Euryale
works metals and sand and heat;
Euryale consults natural philosophers,
seeking crystals that bear no hazes, just smokiness.

DESTRUCTION

Medusa has always had nightmares,
bad dreams, night terrors,
visitations by horrors, memories,
unsettling creatures,
shadows, tricks of light,
tricks of the mind,
some the sea-god but more often
nebulous, amorphous, panic-inducing,
heartrate-escalating episodes of
utter horror.

Athena's face, clear and calm.
Or helmed, with angry eyes.

Deep breaths, hands grasping the sheets,
allowing herself to shake and tremble,
finally letting the calming and calmer
snakes soothe her, and Medusa can
usually go back to sleep
without
the screams
of long ago.
More like a desperate whimper,
say her lovers, the few who

will spend the entire night
with her, the few who trust her
eyes to remain closed or covered,
having made friends with
the little serpents. Like a scream
still, but one that is locked down
in a tight throat, a mouth that cannot open
wide enough to release the
noise entire.

But while Stheno is treating
Greeks and Georgians and
Circassians in the Safavid Empire,
Medusa's nightmares
become emphatic enough to
resonate not just through her own body,
paralyzing the snakes entirely,
but reach her sisters as well.

Medusa's panicked screams
are like no sound the world—
this world—has ever heard.
They rise and fall like a
tsunami of sound, crashing,
battering, breaking, turning
trees into powder, making even
the oldest gods, the ones so deeply
asleep that only the end of the world

could hope to wake them, turn and
move their feet in their sleep.

The screams bring her sisters to her, and
once again, under cover of night,
Stheno and Euryale carry Medusa away,
cursing Athena, who is nowhere to be
found and yet,
always present.

This is the time of calendrical change and
the Cascadia earthquake;
people are too concerned with the illusion
of losing days
and the realities of devastating
waves and falling mountains
to notice three women traveling the seas
without servants or luggage,
making their way to Greece,
drawn by the beacon of their cave.

They certainly never connect
the global shattering
with the women, although
the Cowichan and Makah and
the Quileute and Kwakiutl
and Huu-ay-aht translated the event into
a nighttime fight
between a thunderbird and a whale:

great beings clashing
in a realm to which neither
truly belonged.
Like the bear of long ago, the gorgons sleep again.
Stheno and Euryale circle their sister,
protecting the protectress, shielding her body
and psyche. They make ointments for Medusa's
palms, ravaged by her own nails, brew tisanes
to bring good sleep.
Medusa, exhausted by terror, sleeps the longest,
the hardest. In their old cave by the sea,
Euryale and Stheno wake, talk, return to sleep,
have countless dreams.

Finally, Medusa wakes. Fear of traitorous goddesses
imprisons her,
so she remains secluded
while Stheno and Euryale go away
to scout the situation,
as they once scouted for hunting.

Stheno reports, bringing hummus
and warm bread and olives.
She offers a silent prayer to Chronos,
grateful for time, which destroys all things,
and for the chthonic, where gorgons can safely hide.

Older sisters confer. They weep and sigh,
and soon depart. Euryale promises soon,
soon, a new way to see.

Medusa, alone to test herself,
dresses in new clothes, bought at the market,
covers her snakes with a bright cloth,
covers her eyes, and step by small footstep
slips into the throng.

Her need for violence,
retribution, revenge,
reprisal, retaliation
is eased, just a bit. Long nights in caves
and the decay of the world
drive her to investigate
before a fight.
She learns new sounds, reshaping her palate
as a sculptor shapes clay
assimilating, stressing the ssssss
as her tiny snakes do.

At the dark of the
new moon, Medusa feels
a compulsion. She
sets a plate at a crossroads:
fish seasoned with saffron and garlic,
drinks, and desserts of honey.
A soft breeze

brings Hecate and her hound,
affectionate and comfortable.
The goddess brings a gift from Euryale:
lenses for Medusa's eyes,
objects of enormous power.
She tells a story:
Euryale called on Hecate,
the goddess of three, offering her
a similar feast, and treats
for her dogs, and a request:
could Hecate connect the sisters gorgon
on this night, pass thoughts and matter
between them? She could.

When the skies refresh,
she remains, but she is not
unchanged.
Medusa can view the world
without stopping it.

And she rejoins it,
not as a sea-god or war goddess,
but as a woman, first wary but curious,
then incautious and inexhaustible.
She becomes a queen, an abbess, Joan on her white charger.
She is a Madonna, a ghost, a mistress.
She becomes a slave, an arms-runner, a doxy.

She appears as a man, as a dragon, as a rider on a golden horse.
She is an actress, a scholar, a suffragette.
She works as a miner, a secretary, an enforcer for a mob.
She becomes a starlet, a celebrity, a professor.

MEDUSA ACADEME

It's only been recently
that she's decided to stop hiding
from the world,
from the people who would hunt her
for sport,
for politics,
for trophies
(and how her head would make a lovely one
as demonstrated by a confused
Perseus oh so long ago).
She knows so much
and it was so easy to
finish a PhD
in France—
of course—
where she was welcomed
like the star she is
and fêted and fed
and made even more fabulous
than she already was
by couturiers
and besides, she could stay with her sister
Euryale while she did it.
And then off on a tour—
everyone wanted to book her—

often alone but sometimes
with Warner and Atwood
who became Mar and Peggy
and they all liked the same cocktails, so why not?

She was courted and bribed
but never threatened, no,
never that, no,
and she chose a little college—
or what she calls a little college—
in New England,
where she likes the leaves and the snow
and the swan boats and baseball,
if in an abstract kind of way,
and established herself.

She still does loads of interviews,
loads,
and people flock to her classes
and she is so patient
with so many of them.

This interview made her famous
because of the violence
and because when the police
were asked why her summary judgments
were allowed,
they simply smiled at the reporters

and said she was joking
and no one ever followed up again.

The interview:
(It's with a famous glossy magazine, with smart and astute writers, recently
political, you know the one; young women and older women and clever
people everywhere are reading it. Medusa's pride in its attention wraps
around her, a soft enormous coat. Too bad Athena is such a narcissist to
have alerts for her own name in print, for once she sees it, she reads it too,
and her reawakened anger towards Medusa propels the rest of our tale.)

Medusa wakes and
wraps her hair, coiling the coils
under, blinding them.

Or at least that's what the students think. I know, because
at least once a semester some kid tries to imagine my morning routine
for their final creative writing project, and the instructors like to show me.

It's not too far off.

I have a nice set of turbans for everyday.
I could shave my head, but
the snakes take a while to grow back,
and they really itch while they do.
They only grow about four inches long,
like well-kept dreads.
I guess they are dreads, in a literal sense.
I like the peach turban best; it goes with my complexion well.

But the snakes are blind anyway.
Otherwise they'd be such a nuisance,
hissing at every butterfly or basketball player,
grabbing at things in the supermarket.
They're just there to shock. Silly things. Stupid Athena.

I do have to cover my eyes.
In the 80s, I wore fashionable sunglasses:
Ray-Bans; they used to advertise
with vampires to lure in the goth crowd.
But then I found colored contacts worked,
and I could go swimming in them.
Mine are plain brown.
I get them on the internet,
since I can't see an eye doctor.

Last Monday my class had to have The Talk:
what I have is a disability, not a superpower.
Students and I have this talk frequently.
It's no secret who I am, I'm right there on the
faculty web page: Greek Language and Literature,
dual appointment with Anthropology.
Not a superhero. No superpowers. It's a curse.
But then we have to talk about disability studies:
let's not call it a curse, says one well-meaning
young woman. It's just—Difference.
Where are you placing your accent? I ask, but she doesn't get it.
Eventually they believe me.

My chair doesn't really get it, but the dean does.
I want to get tenure here and stay,
so I have to work them both.
My chair does Latin American folklore.
He doesn't want to think of the chupacabra as a dog
with a disability
or something.
So we avoid the issue.

My dean has a little crush on me,
I think. He always asks about my sisters,
what I'm doing on the weekend.
Grading, I say. Sometimes that's even true.
But I also like to go out.
I go to the nightclubs where my students go,
and I watch them.
Keep an eye out, so to say.

Fine, if you have to ask.
That linebacker who left school last month?
He tried to rape a woman
majoring in economics in the
parking lot of the club on Maple Street.
The one downtown where the bouncer
does too much coke? Yeah, that one.
I was wearing sunglasses, I always do
when I'm out patrolling.
(Yeah, it sounds a little too *Buffy* to me, too.
But whatever.)

Well, what? Mr. Linebacker is still there.
They have a gravel parking lot, you know.
And my name does mean "protectress."
They forget that part.
But I don't.

She places each lens
into her lovely grey eyes,
and watches, guarding.
End of Interview.

She loves her interviews
and she loves telling stories.
There are always stories
in her classes and the students
learn to tell stories too:
in Greek or in pretty English
and they learn the stories of the past
and they tell stories about what students
in the future might tell about them
and their professor.

Mr. Linebacker had no comment,
but he was also recuperating
from the loss of his right arm.
A car accident, he said.

Did I tell you about the time
I gave a lecture on eros

at the ear-piercing place
in the mall? asks Professor Medusa
and even if they have heard it a dozen times,
every student says no! and off she goes.
There's one about chocolate and GIs
in Germany at the end of World War Two
and there's one about learning the sitar.
There's an especially funny one
about Salman Rushdie and bourbon
but truth be told Duse stole that from
a friend, a Shakespearean, almost equally famous.

She rarely tells stories of battle or war or sex
but you know she has some epic ones,
and cute stories
about baby snakes and grasshoppers
are perfectly satisfying.

You
should be dead
and somehow I will bring you to it,
Athena swears at her former priestess,
from a place far away. But she is
achy in her anger;
it's pulling on her shoulders,
her jaw hurts.

During office hours and very early mornings,
Duse writes down stories

about the meaning of masculinity
in translations of the Odyssey,
and think-pieces about modern-day Cyclopes,
and anonymously tweets about
Polyphemus's dick,
and shares pictures of the
coyote-dog-wolf who sometimes
accompanies her on her hunts.
(Hunt details never go on Twitter, though,
no no.)
Brooks Brothers has blocked her because
of too many annoying posts about
the Golden Fleece,
but she does have a circle of followers
who have no idea who she is
besides a humanities professor
in America,
telling stories and persisting.

She loves nice office supplies
and comforting students.
She grades with green ink, so that
students are less stressed when they read
her comments on their essays,
asking for more detail,
correcting citations.

She has a plant in her office,
and a painting of a minotaur; she jokes

that he's her brother. She keeps hand lotion
in her desk and a ball of yarn
and cough drops and a serrated knife
for slicing soft fruit.

She goes to drama department events and
sometimes gives little master classes in projection
and presence. She loves poster day and asks each student
questions. She walks in Take Back the Night and
is a campus escort one night a week, walking
students to their dorms, the library, a lecture.
She shows classic movies on Thursdays during
the autumn term, and cartoons in the spring.
She donates to the student emergency fund;
sometimes she is the student emergency fund.

She teaches with large gestures and long scarves
in dozens of colors at once
and brings in oil lamps
and arrows
and singers from the music department
to recreate ancient life for her students.
They have a feast after exams, all genders together:
wheat tagenites and figs, sesame and honey.
Hers are the best chestnuts they have ever tasted.
There is goat cheese and swordfish,
barley and garum.
And there is fish and saffron and garlic
and honey, lots of honey for

Hecate in case she wants to drop in.
 She grades quickly, always a fast reader.
When she gives out praise,
her voice is full of little cymbals;
she only chides
with her eyes,
so carefully coated with plastic.

Medusa's days follow basic patterns:
rise early and go to school,
come home late,
hunt,
sleep
in the very darkest hours
where above her pillow
is a crown of stone
where her snakes warm or cool
themselves
as she rests.

She dreams so vividly
that sometimes she has to call up a sister
and ask
was that a thing that happened, for real?
And in the middle of the night she can be
sure to her very bones that
she has a rabbit hutch on the porch
and needs to bring a vegetarian potluck
to the meeting tomorrow,

or that she once had wings
but lost them,
possibly in Saratoga
with an unlucky roll of the dice—
she can see the dice, a six and a two—
and she thinks she even remembers the carpet
in her hotel room
from a trip she never took.

Sometimes in her dreams, she's stayed mortal,
her toenails rough and broken and dirty
from working in a field, or
a dream gives her a sudden
and completely true-feeling memory
of her favorite dress from 1682 that was made of
silk and how it looked in the sun in a room
which has never existed.

She has one dream she tries to banish
or logic herself out of even in her sleep,
and in that one she's climbing stone stairs
to a wide open area
and she hears a wave behind her
and suddenly cannot move her feet;
the water has attacked them and she is frozen
in warm salty water and her heart thunders
and she falls
hard
onto the steps

or wakes
sitting up saying
what the hell?

and has to breathe
breathe
breathe

breathe, Medusa

before she can even make her body lie down
again and become soft
and fall back asleep.
Sleep tells stories,
but not always ones Medusa wants to know
and sleep tells lies and sleep tells riddles
and one night when she has been sleeping well,
sleep brings a story worse than the arrival of Poseidon,
worse than the cracking of teeth and cartilage on stone.

The Nightmare for Three Sisters, Stheno calls it,
later, much later,
always pronouncing the capital letters
as if it were a work of art:
a play by Angelou,
a piece by Zwilich.

Athena helps send it; she goes to old allies.
That this insufferable gorgon should be so

successful
when she should be *ashamed* and even more than
ashamed, she should be
dead.

THE NIGHTMARE FOR THREE SISTERS

He is in a form she has never seen, herself:
a bull, with hair like foam,
swirled and thick and caught up
with flotsam. As he moves closer,
she can see that the foam is littered
with dark bones, minuscule bodies
of men and horses: sacrifices and murders,
debts and worshippers, deniers and fanatics.
Although she cannot make out their faces,
Medusa knows that the gods over whom
Poseidon has trampled hang in his fetlocks,
their hair and nails grown long
and brambled as they cling, wet and eroding,
to his legs.

He simply appears in the dreamdark,
walking towards Medusa, who is struck
fast, without air or movement, standing
as she stood in the temple the night
he came ashore. Now it is worse: the bull
signifies something different,
something more brutal than
just—there it is again, Medusa thinks,
her mind flailing for purchase in sanity—just
rape.

The bull-head snorts, a sound to
topple mountains, and a single hoof
falls, almost delicately, but with the
sound of thousands of nails on chalkboards,
wrenching sonic unevenness and Medusa's
eyes, uncovered, shutter and open and twist
and spasm and for a terrifying moment she
is utterly without sight and still cannot breathe,
cannot move, only hear and smell and taste,
and what she hears is the clang of
spear upon shield, spear upon shield,
a metal bang bang bang closing in
coming closer
closer
close.

When she is allowed to inhale again,
to see, to move, Medusa is in a stadium,
the Panathenaic games before her.
Her distance vision is blurred,
but she can see all too well
what is close.
To her right sits Athena, wearing a cloak of
owl feathers, her eyes bright to the point of
mindless absorption in the competition.
To her left is Poseidon, who holds a tankard
of drink in each hand and upon whose bare chest
is painted a large "P."

Poseidon cheers as if
urging a team to victory. Athena
turns her head unnaturally far around and gazes
into Medusa's eyes. Athena's mouth is beakish,
pointed; she contains her rage,
trying to appear in control, above it all,
cool:

I am tired of you. I am tired
of trying to shame you. I am tired of
yelling at you. I am tired—
I have done things the right way
and you have not and I am tired
of having to remind you.
I resisted Hephaestus.
You were supposed to be strong.
Poseidon and I have our quarrels,
but you are certainly not part of them.
You are a gadfly.

I am wisdom. You are a monster.
I am a warrior. You are a whiny brat.
I inspire the divine. You...
her hand makes a circular motion,
meaning, *are nothing.*
Go away and die.

If I have to break your mind,
I will do it,
Athena says.
I am tired of trying to speak to you directly.

Poseidon stands,
roaring and roaring
like an ocean,
a lion,
an elephant seal,
like the sun screaming with fire,
like engines revving to run someone down,
like the wind,
like a bull,
like all of the oceans he commands,
like a bull gaur, sleek enormous power—

and the athletes and musicians
in the stadium's deep pit
become bulls, multiplying in hordes
to fill the space,
white rage and fury,
roiling and rolling
and forcing themselves forward,
seacaps seeking to trample,
to drown,
to bury, to cut through,
to destroy—

and the sacrificed oxen,
given to the hecatomb,
rise, skeletal and dragging
flesh,
like Polynices's corpse,
torn and filthy,
bloodied and dead,
yet staggering,
and swept up by the living bulls,
carried on the seafoam
of their necks and polls,
pushing and racing and surging—

Athena laughs, a funny birdish laugh,
and looking at Medusa again
blinks slowly, once,
and is gone, a mist untouched
by the great tide of bulls
and carrion oxen
who come to destroy Medusa—

and they are running over her
running and running
sharp hooves dig into her body
her breastbone shatters
snakes are ripped away
and a harsh, rising water keeps her down
trying to penetrate
in every way it can

as the dead oxen trip and fall
the odor and feel
of decaying flesh
lying on her own
and the running never stops
and the water forces its way in
and—

awake, gasping for air,
beating at her own body
with her hands, trying to repel
the assault,
checking each delicate snake
for harm,
gasping, gasping.
Her bed is soaked with sweat,
her snakes are limp and exhausted,
her clothes are ripped apart;
Medusa cannot sleep again
for days. And when she does,
the nightmare comes again,
always the same.
She cannot hold against it.

EURYALE'S EYES

It's not a long flight from Paris to Athens,
the city whose name I still hate to say:
I twist it out, a sneer, mocking: oh, this great city
with the name of our tormentor,
with the name of your goddess but our worst goddamned
bully, the one who wouldn't stop even to find hateful words
but went straight to her weaponized body,
the one who could not see truth,
who could not see her way to compassion,
who could not see herself as the very instrument,
of the institutions she wanted to break and remake,
who could not apologize,
who is all to blame. Athens,
scoff, athens, little a, no respect, how I loathe you.

We've all had the dreams now and there is no debate:
Athena, once powerful, then mythologized and reduced
to a story that could be told to little children, that Athena, yes,
is surely wielding power once again. She's read the interview;
newly furious about her failure to end the life of her
once-priestess, she's committed to using that power
to drive us mad
for while no one can kill us,
we can each can decide to end our own lives.
But we gorgons do not waste time:

just as we have settled into post-mythological lives and mundanity,
so we would like Athena to stop hurling
past traumas into our present lives.
Better yet, she should learn from the modern world. It's not perfect,
but with the right guidance, she could
help repair the world.

Seriously, we have all had enough therapy because of that goddess.

I thought we'd worked our way through it all. I thought we—individually
and as a sister-trio—could move beyond what she did. We've come to
          grasps
with betrayal and trust issues and lost time—oh gods the lost time!—I
could still almost weep for those years we spent
hiding, sleeping away swollen eyes and the pain of everyday pricks
like being stabbed with a common fork
in our eyes and our throats and our abdomens. Damned Athena,
why can't you just fucking leave us alone, leave Duse alone
to be her own most badass queen-self in her academic kingdom,
leave Stheno in suburbia
to be the fierce and gentle hunter who heals,
the fierce and gentle healer who hunts,
let me—
let me, dammit, think about eyes and sex and the occasional
gallery opening and funding girls' educations. Leave us alone.
You want power—my boarding pass, yes,
yes, it's Doctor, no, not Madame, no, Doctor, yes, it's Greek—
fucking hell, let me get on the plane—
power? For what now? Would you kill

or condemn rape victims some more? Look how well that turned out.
Is shaming victims somehow apotropaic for you? Do the bodies
of women and children protect you from others seeing your
flaws, your rigid hate?

I will tear her shields down, her armor,
I will tear Medusa's face from her arms,
I will take her helmet from her head and cleave her brains with
          weapons that
I will forge myself from coins bearing her face, and I will—yes, please,
          red—
I will drown her still-breathing body and send her to Poseidon in bundles
smaller than owl pellets.

Breathe, self. Breathe.

Gods, how I wanted her to be wise and just and for Medusa to love her.
For that, even I would have carried water for her feet or made armor for her
          horse's tail;
I would have fought for her and done her laundry and kissed
those she had embraced with the heat of the hottest day
and I would have crawled up mountains for her and down into the
          underworld;
I would have torn my own arms off for her and sewn them back with
          eyelashes;
oh, how I wanted her to be what she was supposed to be.

I cannot sigh enough to express myself about my disappointment—
not to mention—
now—
my cynicism.

She wasn't, though.
I couldn't know that, then.
All I knew was what we all knew: what the
gods' propagandists told us:
Athena Atryone, untiring,
Parthenos, virgin—what a stupid concept to believe in and value in the first
        place, virginity—
Promachos, fighting in front,
Polias—of the city—and Pallas—weapon and warrior—and
Ergane—industrious. And judge, woman of horses,
gentler of horses, diver, swimmer,
ship-builder, ship-guider, ship-wright's goddess.
Hygieia, health. Tritogeneia, born of water, triple-born of the world.
And bright-eyed, bright-eyed Athena, Athena Glaukopis.

I looked into her eyes, her silver, gleaming, quick eyes
and through her, I fell into eyes forever.
Everyone's eyes are my eyes now; I see everyone's eyes
and her eyes, animal and human together,
were diminished early: grey falling to clouds,
the blue-green sea that lay within them turning dark,
conflicted, cataract-filled with anger and confusion.
Her eyes became unnatural,
not of any part of the world,

blotted and flecked with occlusions,
unable to see with clarity literal or metaphorical.

I warned Medusa, I tried to tell her:
how could a goddess embody health when she killed?
How could a goddess claim to be just and trick others into suffering?
But Medusa believed: she had even more desire than I did
to serve and to serve; and
to serve this goddess, to overlook the gleam of anger in her eyes,
to try to reconcile or brush away the contradictions and
the hypocrisy that made war wise and petty fights heroic.

After Athena's betrayal of Medusa, her own sworn priestess,
and after she made Perseus a hero for killing a victim of her own rival,
Poseidon sea-god, after we fooled her, after after after all that—
she left us alone.

For a time, anyway, but not enough.

Perhaps she didn't want anyone to know that Medusa survived,
that Perseus was a robotic killer without a mind of his own,
that gorgons in the sea-cave remained—quiet, but alive.
She went about her business: lying to men, disguising herself
and tricking her worshipers, cursing musical instruments, blinding
accidental stumblers, transforming her challengers into animals,
scheming and manipulating gods and demigods and non-gods all alike.

By the time we entered the world again,
the temple serpents were dead, their honey cakes left untouched to

crumble in the rain and fly away in the wind.
While we survived and took on new dress and accent and food,
new names and professions and histories,
she had become myth, sleeping deeply.

Scores of paintings and sculptures
did not revive her,
but kept her in that artist's box
of deities passé, unruly
and untrustworthy
gods with lives of scandal
and absurdity.

Just some water, please.
Technically, I'm on an extended research and humanitarian aid trip;
if I'm not back in a year—and neither are my sisters—
my assistants will shut down my Paris practice.
It is only that Athena
sees fit to torment us, Duse in particular, that we
make this trip: some fanaticism,
a misplaced feminism,
a new interest in old gods
feeds this one
that she has the strength to send us such dreams.

We will find out.
Once again, with no fanfare or heraldic procession,
the sisters gorgon enter Attica. Well.
I do, anyway. Stheno should be on a plane with Duse.

As for Duse, after that interview,
she is lucky to be unbothered
in her small New England haven,
on her way to the airport,
not surrounded by town and gown offering both
pitchforks and rescue,
shouting down her purported stonings of rapists and
gospelling her rock-strewn crusade,
pitting her own violence against that of the men—
it's usually men—
who attack the women she wants to protect.

She has made herself into a goddess-protector—
the very kind we all wanted Athena to be: a woman with
power beyond the physical or political who would
cherish us, guard us against unwanted marriages or
forced motherhood or any predations. Medusa
is no goddess—and she rightfully declaims it
on a regular basis to everyone—but a promachos,
the warrior at the front lines, she has gained followers
and supporters
and will one day soon gain
foes.

Like Batman, she will always be a vigilante.

She probably likes to think of herself as being like Batman.
I would.

There have always been cults of Athena, small groups
of women to whom she represents female agency.
They don't seem to know her full history though:
she has never helped other women, never saved them,
never shielded them, no: she has always been the protector
and champion of the patriarchy. Sisters, wake:
her womanhood does not make her your ally.

ARRIVAL

Homecave, seawater, a lamp, food.
Three as one, slipping between time and non-time.
Rest. Thought.

In the benevolent dark and half-light
of their homecave,
gorgon sisters eat olives and small silver fish.
They sleep, and dream of nothing.
They talk, and speak of Athena.
They go into the world and find information.
Assumptions are unfurled and
like ancient dust, blown away.
Athena's power comes
from a tiny sliver of
renewed mortal worship,
but more from mortal judgment propagated
on her own poor judgment:
a god said a victim should be shamed,
and the people took that idea
and ran with it.

Those runners have become
a tide of ignorance
and loathing,
and Athena, not knowing

of more compassionate
thought,
is fueled by it,
waking to its warmth
and finding Medusa
a still-present
and perfect
target.

If she had made me like this,
says Medusa, to be a weapon
against the violence of men,
I would still remain her devotee.
Euryale shakes her head: Athena
made you a monster because she did not
listen to you, or any woman. She believed
so much in Olympus's woman-hating,
male-made myths of the body and mind, that
she never questioned any of it: she sent that fool
Perseus to kill you.
Perseus carried your head—or rather,
our ensorcelled simulacra thereof—
all over the place, bragging about his kill,
bragging about Athena's support of his actions.
Oh, his bragging! Remember the curse we put
on the head? His bragging led to vast lack
of power in so many ways.
He was happy to take credit for all sorts of things:
Andromeda's seven children, for example.

What? asks Medusa.

Not his, replies Euryale. Stheno bursts out laughing.
Our curse worked well.

Here is what it comes to, says Euryale,
pacing the cave.
Athena and Poseidon are rivals for this city.
Athena wins over the people of the city.
You—pointing at Duse—consort with the enemy—
in *her* mind. In the real world, where we live,
Athena's great rival rapes you.
From Athena's warped point of view—
being the daughter of the world's most
prolific rapist and rape apologist has got
to fuck you up, especially when he's your only parent—
(why do you think Artemis asked Zeus to keep men away from her?
Oh gods, Artemis, says Medusa, we could go on all day—
She at least punished the perpetrators! Stheno says. Not the victims.
Medusa leans her head against her sister's shoulder,
and Stheno encircles her arms around her,
letting the uncovered snakes tap against her cheek and jaw.)

May I continue? asks Euryale, impatient. Yes, from
Stheno, gently rocking Duse.

No, says Duse. And let's not forget that Artemis is jealous.
You have to be careful with her.
She's not just all goodness and light—that whole thing with Callisto—

That was Hera who changed her into a bear, says Euryale. Now focus.
Can we get back to the present?

Stheno and Medusa eat olives and
save the pits in
a little wooden bowl. Stheno
strips leaves from a vine
and adds them to the pits.
Her fingers stir in a triangular pattern:
three, three, three always.

Euryale continues:
So, Medusa is raped by Athena's rival, and instead of attacking
Poseidon, Athena attacks Duse, first making her deadly, and then
sending destructo-boy after her.

But why is she coming after you now? Euryale asks
in a rhetorical tone, she feels empowered again—
men are giving her ideas power.

How do we stop it?

If I knew that, I wouldn't be in this cave,
says Medusa. A snake hisses, a tiny little hiss,
but righteous all the same. I'd be at home,
with a drink, grading. But when I think about
being out there—I don't know what she's capable of.

...capable of, says Stheno. How can she be capable

of anything? She should be going to the
grocer and baker and working a job,
like the rest of us. Or don't Olympians
do that?

She was a goddess before us, sister,
and always more powerful than three
minor figures. Duse has the most power
of us all—she became immortal and
has held onto it.

We heal, says Stheno, but Euryale brushes
this away, a fly among fruit.

No, listen—Duse says, sitting up, animated—she's right:
gorgons heal.
If Athena plagues me—
plagues us—
can we cure ourselves
of her?
Can we
disinfect ourselves
of her?
I had it out with Poseidon
long long ago
and he leaves me alone—
he's not an infection—
but she—
she is.

Inoculating one's self against a goddess of old
seems a rather academic and semantic point to Euryale.
But to get her to see reason, that may well work:
Justitia favors reason over emotion, after all.
Athena's in our heads, not our blood; but
surely somehow we can entreat that facet of her godhood.

Perhaps, muses Stheno. And we can't do it alone.

But! says Medusa. There is strength in numbers,
yes?
Isn't that what people say?
We have numbers, sisters,
oh
we have numbers.

Which is how the gorgons came to host a party.

STRENGTH IN NUMBERS

Three sisters arrive first,
these oft-tricked by hubristic men,
daughters of Nyx who give off,
paradoxically and resplendently,
great banners of light.
The Hesperides are glad to leave
their little garden, where they must
spend their days tending
apples of immortality,
playing with an easily-bored
dragon, and currying favor with
Hera.

Indeed, Hera accompanies them,
followed by the puppy-like
Ladon, who cavorts
and tumbles and leans on
everyone's legs, begging for
attention and petting behind his
great floppy scaly ears.

I thought you were running
some kind of
hearth-home
bullshit group,

Hera,
says Euryale.

The goddess sighs
deeply and
the corner of her mouth
twitches
unhappily.
I changed my mind,
she says.
The nymphs invited me,
I can go if you don't—
no, says Euryale, but
what are you doing here,
now?

I—
she closes her eyes
and puts up her hands
defensively—
I do other things,
now. I—
I teach self-defense
and anti-harassment training
and—

Hera! says Stheno
putting her arm around the
shorter woman.

Euryale,
did you know that Hera's
foundation paid for
the processing of six thousand rape kits
last year?
A round-faced woman
pops up on the other side of Hera.
Io! says Stheno,
I heard you two were working together,
waggling her fingers at the two women:
Zeus be damned, am I right?

Euryale's eyebrows assume heights
unknown to mortals
and her beautiful mouth
falls ever so slightly
open.

Let me get you some drinks,
says Stheno, who has already had
a few herself, relaxing
and not having to be forgettable
for the first time in many years.

More trios and triads arrive:
Thriae, Naxians, Mysians,
Asterionides.
Quartets and quintets
and solo travelers:

hamadryads and naiads,
happy maenads bringing
boxes of wine and
skins of ouzo.

Ladon is the favored guest
until at last he stretches out,
scales on stone,
and sleeps, his long
whiskers gently rising
and settling like the sun.

Hera has lived a long life
under the eye and hand and body
of her worthless husband and
itches for disruption: she leans up
against Ladon's back
next to lovely big-eyed Io
and takes out a notebook.

While Arethusa makes a dinner
of fish and seaherbs over the
light of her own hands, and as
Aegle reaches her mind through
cavewall mist
and sea-caressed stone to
contact and gather yet more allies,
Erytheia lays out the sisters' offerings.
Before we make a plan,

she says,
I'll give you an
inventory:
orange-pink apples, which do far more than make
the eater immortal
(they also make you dizzy but give you good skin
and yet make you irritable around crowds
but enable you to get by on almost no sleep);
Perseus's ill-gotten carrying case
designed to hold Medusa's head;
and the Hesperides' combined powers of
illumination,
dazzlement strong enough to blind a man,
a glowing heat that immolates,
and the most secret light,
commanded by Erytheia:
a sharp, precise beam:
a guide, a weapon, a space opera
icon.

Stheno nods. Not sure
we'll need any of that, she says,
stretching out the words,
but you never know.

Nymphs and gods eat together.
Like any friends—or at least those
who share communal pasts and myths—
they catch up.

Nemesis lurks about but is ignored,
as are the Erinyes; finally
Euryale
puts them in a grotto
and tells them that their
particular skills,
which might *seem* perfect
for getting Athena to leave
Medusa alone,
are not needed, but that they themselves are
always welcome. They fall to discussion
and upon finding a common interest
in skin care, happily pass the evening.

FOLD UP YOUR WINGS

There is dessert and then the Hesperides
decide it's time
to get to business.
Euryale finds it funny that they have taken charge,
but who is she, she thinks, to argue?
I don't think we need to wait,
one tells her sisters:
others will arrive when they arrive.

Fold up your wings, sisters,
come together and hear me,
begins Aegle.
We can't undo the past,
but we can
protect the protectress
Medusa.
To know our way forward,
we must
know the past,
and in doing so
turn past to path,
moving from violence
to serenity.

Athena, sending Perseus to us, did
fail us too, Aegle tells the assembly.
Erytheia jumps in: As did Heracles, her erstwhile minion,
who yet garners fame and worship—
—as a cartoon, says Duse wryly—
even so, persists the nymph, people worship
him:
a murderer,
a rapist,
a braggart. Protected by
Athena.

The patron goddess of heroes,
says a quiet voice in a cave shadow,
why did we ever think of them as such?
Hecate steps lightly and sits amidst
the other women. She reaches out to
Medusa, and the gorgon's snakes twine
themselves in pleasure around the goddess's
hand, their little mouths curved like
human smiles.

Hera tenses, but sleeping Ladon
reassures her, and she nods across the cave;
Hecate smiles back. Truces must be made
if Athena is to be reckoned with.

As the Hesperides speak,
Pale Dawn comes, bringing

Melissae, their outlines blurred
with fuzz and pollen;
Charities, more triplets,
lead the Graeae.
The Moirai arrive as one,
embrace only Ladon, and
sit in a corner the cave has
just made for them,
spinning, measuring, cutting
without pause.

Medusa stares at them openly until
Atropos sighs, her hands holding
a cradle of threads,
and breaks the meaning of her name:
I am not always so unturnable, she admits:
we were wrong
to aid
so many monsters,
demigods,
men.
We atone

We atone.

We atone.

Spindle scratches stone and
all eyes focus on the trio—

neither old nor visibly disabled—
and Stheno speaks:
You are at our hearth.
You bring your work with you;
you can make the gods conform,
but what will you do for those wronged
by them?

Lachesis pauses in her measuring
and her sisters stop their tasks.
We cannot bring you the Keres,
she says, I have already measured the
lives of the gods.
Their threads thicken and become thin:
many have wound down to a single hair—
their lives are so fine and rare now,
sustained only by children
and the desperate and the delusional.
Athena's thread is so light—she is
sustained by women who do not
understand her cruelty,
who think cruelty between
women is honorable.

Hera nods, but
looks only at her feet,
warmed by the hearth
made by other women
until Io pushes against her shoulder,

reassuring.
Lachesis continues: what you
want to fight is thought—
Athena's ideals that perversely
fight against time and rationality.
She waves a hand in the air
without seeming to move.

We are irrational constructs, she says,
her wide sleeve sailing across the corner
of the cave. Athena's thread will never
end. All you can do is make it
thinner, almost invisible.

We will raise up new gods! says a nymph:
We will put up statues
and altars and we will serve and sacrifice—
Gods are not the answer, says Euryale.
We are definitely not, echoes a new voice.
Artemis stands in the entryway,
her feet in shadow.

Artemis's hounds sniff around the sleeping Ladon
and return to her, tongues flopping. They stand at her side,
lie at her feet. One sits on her toes, others chase shadows,
so silent as to be hallucinations,
around the walls of the seacave.

To bring back old gods, says Artemis,
matter-of-factly,
is to bring back old
tragedies,
jealousies,
rivalries,

punishments,
challenges,
contests.

I could bring those back for you—
I could return in a chariot
drawn by five wild deer
crowned with antlers of soft gold
and summon child priestesses
to play the bear in the old rites,
oh,
I could do those things.
Hera could do the same,
Hecate, the same, yes, more people
dream of you than you would think possible.
Check your threads, Fates, and show them
their unending faint lives and mine. Clotho
knows well how to add to a thread; she has done it before.
But I too did cruel things.
She seems to look Hera in the eye,
but to address them all.
Unspeakable harms

I wish I could undo,
but the thread is always pulled
in one direction only;
as an old god, a powerless god,
a god existing on the thinnest hair,
how do I atone? And beyond atonement,
how do I learn the ways of a new world?

The world out there is gullible, says Euryale:
people want to believe in things. Easy things:
that giving up a bird or singing a chant
or making money will give them
what they want: solace? Righteousness? A place in
a mythical—she laughs—afterworld?

Hera raises a hand, a student,
hoping to speak, and then does:
I went to the world,
she says, penitent. I was like
an infant, immersed in things
and ideas I could not
fathom.
I went to Lethe and drank away
my old self and all I did and believed,
and I let my sister Hestia
place me in a home
in the world.

Three times now I have done this,
Hera testifies, standing. And each time
when I come of the age of reason
Mnemosyne restores my knowledge
of what all I did before.
Only now do I think I am
of a season, of experience,
of knowing that I can
create real sanctuaries
for women,
places of protection,
ways of power.

I am older than warrior gods.
I have been used and I have used
and I have been branded jealous
for resisting being used.
What I do now may seem small
to goddesses and gorgons,
but it is a path
from the past
to power.

Medusa stands and stretches
and the snakes shift about,
still reveling in the attention
of Hecate, sleepy and content
in the warmth of the cave.
They want symbolic things

they can pretend are real, says the professor.
The cave is so full of nymphs and dryads
and goddesses, even bright Echidna, a water-goddess
whose shimmering rivers are long diminished,
that were they not all
in their own ways immortal
surely oxygen would be
running out.
What does Athena want?
There is only the sound of the sea,
and Ladon, snoring gently.

We may be immortal, Stheno finally says,
looking at the shadows on the wall,
dancing in fire,
tiptoeing around the sea entrance to the cave,
but I at least am used to sleep.
Stay—everyone—I have
enchanted our space
with gifts of Athena to the city,
turned back against her,
that we should be unknown to her,
but welcoming and healing
for those in need.
Olive pits, fragrant and
gem-like,
dot the cave floor.

Medusa is up all night.

CAVELIGHT AND SEAMORNING

When the morning rises,
Dero and Tithorea and Halimede
are talking about Studio Ghibli movies
with Hecate
and
Polydora and Metope have found
a Greek hip hop radio station
and
Strophia is telling Ampelos about
photography
and the cave is lit
gently
with the glow of
supernatural happiness
and hazelnut-sized
lights conjured
from hands and horns
and like bubbles from mouths
and
Eudora and Phyto and Coronis
bring a shower
to the edge of the cave,
and the waves, trying to keep
Poseidon asleep and unknowing
of this gathering,

lightly tap the
cave entrance,
reflecting early sunlight
into the space
where Stheno stretches and rises,
and where Euryale disentangles
her long dark limbs from similar
extremities and
Medusa is smiling,
clever Duse,
who has been thinking
from nightfall to seamorning.

SAVING FACE

Hera, you are a genius,
says Medusa, her snakes
bopping about her face. She pushes
one away from her eye:
stay up here, buddy, ok?

Hera is generally used to being
shat upon and so
stares at Duse in utter surprise.
She swallows a mouthful of
grilled something and says, What?

Medusa is electric:
Athena has to save face. We have
to save her face. We can't win
if she's humiliated. Duse talks
with her hands, circling
her own
visage
and hovering around her shoulders.
She has to be able to save face.
With Cassandra, oh, the sorry Cassandra—
she did it by wrecking Ajax's ship,
but they were both human,

weak in her eyes,
but I am not.
She has to save face.

Euryale looks at her sister:
Duse, deep breath. Then
explain.

Medusa just grins at her,
an entirely genuine grin.
She's *tired of me*, Duse says.
Tired. She doesn't want to keep doing
this, but she does, because she thinks it's right
but, maybe more importantly,
what would Poseidon or anyone think
if Athena, the great goddess,
were to quit?
Remember Odysseus at
the court of Arete?
Athena sent him there, a stronghold
of Poseidon and Zeus,
because Poseidon loved
them so much that
no matter what they did,
he could not harm them
for hosting that weeping prat
of a wanderer.

Medusa inhales:
Athena can't just quit on me,
her fallen disciple, without
people thinking that she would
quit on anything. What
would she quit next, if she
has quit punishing Medusa?
Would she stop protecting Athens?
Quit being a symbol of wisdom,
quit transmogrifying into large
and often annoying birds?
Quit carrying around a shield
bearing
my God-damned face?

If she admitted that she was wrong
about me,
what else could be
questioned?
People have always
questioned her motives
in and after the Trojan War.

But she can't do this all by
her lonesome self, no,
she needs help. And the question
becomes how do we—Duse gestures, wide
and swinging—do that? Who
can speak with her? Who

does she trust? Who—dammit, I am beginning
to sound like her pet bird—who
can do that? Who can teach her that she's wrong
and that she doesn't have to do this?
Whom does she still prize?

A dog whines and Artemis,
reaching her hand and
quieting it,
says
Pallas.

No, says Hera, I mean
have you ever even seen her?
In any incarnation, in any age,
in any world? I am not even sure
if she existed. She was a dream of
Philodemus, a back-creation, a
ret-conning of Athena's weapon-laden
self.

No, says Artemis. She is
the most hidden of all of
Athena's victims, but she
inheres. She was like Medusa,
a devotee of Athena,
and even more:
not just a foster-sister but
a sworn and equal sister-in-arms.

And of course,
you all know how that ended:
in bouting, Athena killed her.
Oh, Athena said Zeus had distracted her,
it was a big misunderstanding;
Pallas zigged where Athena
anticipated she would zag.
However you know it,
the end was the same:
Athena killed Pallas
with her—she laughs,
a hollow sound, mocking
and angry—*celebrated* spear.

Stheno crosses the cave to
her patron goddess, caressing
the dogs' ears as she passes each one.
She does not quite kneel, but
her body is supplicated nonetheless,
a bow, a kneeling of spirit. Her voice
is low and reverential.
Would she come for us? she asks;
would she come for herself?
I do know about hiding, Stheno continues,
I have known it and my sisters
know it, and we will never
take a hiding woman
from her sheltering place
without her full consent.

And...but...
Euryale begins,
isn't she, you know—
she gestures to the women
circling the cave,
leaning on one another,
heads on shoulders and
arms around waists
and hands on backs
and
knees—
dead-dead?

Seeing raised eyebrows
and concerned looks
from nymphs and
goddesses,
she continues:
she wasn't born immortal,
and here she gestures to herself,
hand on her collarbone, and to
Stheno—and she wasn't somehow
made immortal—here she touches
Duse's nape, and snakes writhe,
happy for contact, against
her hand.
Right?
So....

Artemis nods:
she was mortal.
Athena killed her,
and raised a statue,
and took her name
as an honorific
to...memorialize her.
But her memorial
and name are long gone,
subsumed by Athena,
and whatever ability
Pallas had to make footsteps
on true earth
disappeared. She hides
in the Underworld.

Nymphs and goddesses
look at each other's eyes.
This is a challenge.
They murmur,
and the cave is soon
loud.

Medusa holds up a hand,
stepping forward, quieting all.
Can we not
send to her? Plenty of us

have entered the Underworld and returned
to live many days—Heracles,
Sibyls, some very passionate Bacchae?

Artemis closes her eyes, her hand
still, resting on a hound,
thinking. Her eyes move
beneath her eyelids,
quick and slow.
When she opens them,
the air around her shimmers
with deliberation.
I will send to her,
says Artemis. She kneels
and her hounds surround her,
noses to hers, licking her breath
and swallowing her words.
She speaks so softly
no one can hear,
and then turns to Hecate.
A blessing?
Hecate gives a blessing.
Artemis turns to the Hesperides.
A blessing?
They too give a blessing.
She turns to the gorgons.
I will need, she says,
enumerating,
touching long fingers

with the opposite thumb,
a bone with marrow,
the richest coin you have.
She pauses, and looks sorrowfully
at Medusa. And one serpent.
But Medusa laughs, shaking her head.
That is small change, she says.
They grow back.

This one may not, says Artemis.
It may find a place Underneath,
or it might journey back with
envenomed news. We will see.
She kneels again amidst the dogs
and wraps her arms around three
and when she rises, a new figure rises
with her, a phantom woman
in plain clothes.
Euryale hands her a coin,
Stheno hands her a bone,
and Medusa, taking a small
knife from Hecate,
easily slices away a snake
from her head and hands it
to the phantom.

Almost immediately,
as Medusa predicted,
another begins to grow in

125

its place, and Duse,
despite the growing aura of
sanctity surrounding this
makeshift ritual, rolls her eyes
and gently scratches at it.
It is not quite the same
as its predecessor, though:
it is darker, more chthonic,
than the others. It is coiled,
keeping to itself,
as the other snakes weave
and bob happily among
each other.

The phantom woman bows
to Artemis, Hecate, gorgons,
the assembly, and walks from the cave,
vanishing into light as she goes.
Artemis sighs; now we wait, she says.

Euryale sits and asks Artemis,
have you been there?
Hell no, the god jokes,
and the spell of ritual lifts.
Hera and Dawn pour drinks,
and the party begins anew.

But Euryale wonders, and
draws Artemis aside.

What aren't you telling us?
She looks Artemis in the eye,
even as Aphrodite keeps a keen
eye on Euryale.
Euryale glances back at Aphrodite,
saying, this hiding is extreme,
especially for a mortal
supposedly once loved by
Athena.
It is a matter of love, isn't it?
she presses, reaching to bring
Aphrodite into the conversation.
She holds her patron's arm just so
not disrespectfully, but with pressure.
Artemis looks at Aphrodite,
and the goddess of love
makes a small gesture
with her long fingers and supple hands,
and the trio is encased in silence.
How do you *do* that? asks Artemis.
The game I could hunt if no one could hear me.
Aphrodite smiles. Sometimes you cannot
risk any sound—her eyes widen suggestively—
and lovers know this best of all. But her
face grows more serious, and she takes
Euryale's hand.
Sweet one, you guess too well, she says
and Euryale replies,
lifetimes loving women

have made me at least a little wise.
Athena loved Pallas, and
Athena killed Pallas, and,
shamed by her father,
Athena kept her love secret.
The *shame* she calls for Medusa
is an echo of the shame
her father called for her.

TIME

Time passes,
the light changes.
Seamorning is gone
and gone too are the stars
many times over. The cave
has new light, different light,
light now from Ladon's
enormous
puppy-dog eyes,
light from Duse's serpents,
who glow gently like
children's nightlights,
ever so faint and pale.
Artemis's remaining hounds shift,
their bodies long lines
from ears to tail through
stretched-out backs,
curving slightly, full of
muscle and speed.

Outside the cave, the ocean
is constant, as constant as it can be,
subject to gravity and far-off
fishing boats dragging along home
towards morning

and docks and gulls
yelling in their ears
and cats darting in for guts
and eyes.

Outside, the sky is
almost empty, a generous
cloud covers the moon,
slipping around her like a
cool cotton pillowcase
on plump stuffing,
atop a bed
under a summer fan.

Outside, the air is hot
and the gorgons can't quite
remember the season in which
they came here, other than Duse,
who knows they arrived between
September and June, but time
can be tricky, and cavetime,
especially with so many other
magics and glamours and spells
and residual supernaturality in and
around it, and none know whether
this is a time of harvest or planting
or bathing or sleeping, and Stheno
misses the long-ago blue bear.

Stheno steps out into the sheltered grotto
and her sisters trail behind her. Wrapping
their arms around one another's
waists, youngest Medusa in the center,
they lean their heads on her shoulders
and look to the slow-nighting horizon.

Behind them, Artemis is talking to
Aphrodite:
where are your dogs? she asks,
rubbing a hound's ear. Oh, says
Aphrodite, when I travel I
leave them with Kate Bush.

What if she doesn't come? asks
Medusa, calm and soft.
We'll make other plans,
says Stheno.
We'll figure something out,
says Euryale. We're immortal.
Athena can't kill us—
she can make me want to kill
myself says Medusa,
no longer as calm or soft.
I will make sure, Euryale says,
grimness in her voice, that her
actions against you will end. And
the look she gives Stheno
behind Medusa's lovely,

swaying snakes
is very grim indeed.

I want to swim, says Stheno;
Poseidon doesn't give a damn
about any of us anymore and besides,
we are water goddesses, born of water,
beloved of water.
He can go fuck a shark, says Euryale,
lifting the mood suddenly,
and arms still wrapped around one another,
three gorgons plunge into the sea.
They are soon joined by a dozen
water nymphs
and their own older sisters,
one of whom asks when the last time
their parents surfaced.
Around 1982, says Enyo,
Ceto was trying to keep
all those soldiers away from the
Falklands.
Echidna floats, drowsily,
her tail dragging across
sand and rocks,
and replies
Oh, I saw Phorcys
not too long ago—
when I used the eye
to get updates on

Turkish politics.
Typhon, now, she continues,
I never see him anymore.

He's in America, says
a nearby nymph.
Being windy.
Medusa turns:
he's in *Chicago?*
Nymphs and goddesses
and immortals laugh,
and the sun
rises and sets,
and gorgons
and goddesses
and nymphs
and Ladon
and the hounds
conjure food
and dine on it
and conjure visions
for entertainment
and swim
and wait
and time
moves around them,
the moon circles
its halo
and once more

the party winds down
to sleep once more.

PHANTOM SPEECH

Artemis knows first,
by the movement of her hounds
smelling something both familiar
and not, alert and relaxed,
they move legs into
position, ready to leap,
and draw back their lips
so subtly, no human
could tell to look,
and their haunches
quiver
just so,
the movement of
readying for action,
focused on
the unwieldy phantom
crouched down
at the cave's entrance,
looking for them,
and for her goddess.

Artemis calms the hounds,
a flat hand above them all,
and, knowing her creation,
beckons the phantom to her,

silently, silently,
for others sleep all around,
their aspirations unneeded but
habitual, at least for those
who have lived in the world.

The phantom creeps,
forgetting its form, turning
step by step from
shod human feet into
arched canine toes,
ticking softly, and the entire
grey and beautiful shape
coming undone, arms into legs
and a head into three, and
the torso and shoulders twist
and three dogs, exhausted,
relieved, and happy, but
clearly aged
join the pile
around Artemis.
She holds each one,
strokes their newly
grey ears and
massages their spines and hips.
They close their eyes, clouded over
with distance and sights
they can never tell,
and they lean

companionably
against each other
and the other dogs
and Artemis's warm legs,
and they sleep together,
harriers after hares.

In her sleep,
Artemis
opens her eyes
to another grey figure:
slight, its very outlines
threads caught
by passing winds,
dissipating even as it
stands.

If Medusa the protectress
cannot protect herself,
says the figure,
how can I be protected?
Who will guarantee me safe passage,
to and from?
Who will protect me
when I am gone beyond all
rivers and all gates?
Artemis speaks solemnly.
Athena did not love Medusa,
she says. Athena loved you.

And I will guarantee your safety.
And I will call upon all here
to guarantee your safety.
We will all be your protectresses.

More wisps fly away.
A wind blows.
Wherever they are, it is empty.

I will not meet her in Olympus,
says the Pallas-sending. It is
too powerful and corrupt,
full of the philosophies that
caused my death.

Agreed, Artemis says quickly,
and I do not want your hiding place
disturbed. The meeting will
take place here, on the ground,
of the earth,
where you lived and died, and
which I will sanctify.

I should have protected you then,
Artemis says.
Hebe watches for me now,
as I will never become old,
says the shade. You prepare
a place, and I will ask her

to bring me,
and return me
when we are done.
But if Athena does not
do what you want,
does not see her
hubris,
does not understand,
I will not come again.

The wind blows
and blows into Artemis's eyes
and as she shields them with her arm,
she wakes
in the cave
with sleeping hounds
and charcoal on her hands,
as if she had made a sacrifice
in her own palms.
The other women sleep,
and Artemis draws her
suddenly old hounds closer to her,
and is quiet until the dawn.

HEBE

Sure, says Aegle, I can call Hebe.
Can she meet us here, first, asks Stheno,
and help us figure out where this...
incredibly weird and awkward... meeting
should take place?
They stand on a patch of beach,
newly born for the occasion,
where neither wind nor wave
can interfere with communication.
Ladon has dragged half of his long body
onto it, and he sleeps in the sun, as does
one of Artemis's newly old hounds.
Aegle sits with her toes in the water and
looks out over the sea, green and blue.

Long minutes pass. Stheno turns to Duse:
did you know she did a stint with me
as a neo-natal nurse?
What? says Duse, distracted.
Hebe, says Stheno. She—
never mind.
Aegle's face is blank, unchanging.
Lush eyebrows are still, her lashes
cast shadows on her cheeks.
Finally she speaks. Okay,

she says, standing, brushing sand
from her body. She'll be here tonight.
But you might want to send the
Fates away—they object to the whole
eternal youth thing.
Nah, replies Stheno. The cave is
big enough
for everyone.
Look for an eagle
when the moon
passes the meridian,
says Aegle. Hera will
want to greet her.

For the rest of daylight,
the gorgons and their guests
discuss meeting places
for Pallas and Athena.
Can we even trust her,
asks a nymph. She had kids with
Heracles, her own half-brother.
Yeah, well,
now she's living with a DJ
in Krakow, says another.
What's neutral in this world,
asks another.
Switzerland,
quips Euryale, sitting down
among them

with a glass of wine.
A field in the middle of nowhere,
says Stheno, leaning on
a hound.
Nepal, suggests someone.
Pallas's home turf, says Medusa:
Libya.
Mm, nods a nymph. Pentapolis.
No, says Euryale.
That's not a very safe area now,
especially for women.
But they're immortal,
or already dead, says someone.
I am not going to ask anyone
to go to Benghazi, says
Euryale with a snort.

The moon rises.

Ladon and the hounds sleep
in a heap of scales and fur.
Medusa's eyes are tired;
her snakes sleep, and she longs
to do the same.
But there's a scuffing sound,
and a new voice,
asking
who's awake? hello?

Chocolate? asks the new voice.
Medusa's head wheels around
and finally her eyes land on
the owner of the new voice.
She's small, with tiny short little dreadlocks
and a gold nose ring. She's crouching down
to look at the gorgons and
holding
a candy bar. Chocolate? she repeats.
Thanks? Medusa says. Hebe?

That's me! says the newcomer.
Euryale wakes: I was expecting an eagle,
she says.
Oh, says Hebe, sorry. I changed before
I came in, so not to startle anyone.
Chocolate? Her supply comes from
the air.
Euryale elbows Stheno, who wakes
looking up. Eagle? she asks.
Hebe, says Euryale, with chocolate.
Oh, I knew you'd bring candy,
says Stheno to the goddess. Youth thrives on it,
says Hebe, nodding.
Do you want us to get Hera? asks Stheno.
Nah, says Hebe, I'll find her later.
She sits, cross-legged, a Buddha.
So, she says, you think that if Athena
meets Pallas again, on some neutral ground,

Athena might stop harassing you? She points at
Medusa.
Medusa says:
yep.

Hebe doesn't look convinced.
She pulls out gumdrops and eats
two orange ones and a green one.

What do you really want to happen?
she asks, I mean, how do you hope this
is going to go?

Medusa takes a bit of chocolate.
She gestures as she speaks, her hands
and the chocolate bar moving around.
I want her to feel like she can change,
says Medusa. I want her to understand that she's
harmed people,
that she's ruined lives,
but that she can change,
and that in changing,
she can feel some sorrow
for what she did.
Hebe is skeptical.
Change, she says?
Voluntarily?
Her eyebrows
are eloquent.

Hera did....says Duse.
...and so we thought if Athena
could find a way, without being
humiliated....that if Pallas asked....

Okay, says Hebe without judgment,
standing up and brushing her hands
together.
Where and when?

Where would Pallas feel most safe? asks Stheno.
Hebe thinks, stretching out her feet.
No place in our worlds, certainly, she says.
Zerzura? Ciudad Blanco? she says.
No way, Stheno replies quickly:
Immortal doesn't mean immune to mosquitoes.
Euryale looks at them all.
Avalon, she says. Artemis has been there.
Avalon will be safe for both.
No one there worships them;
it's all women; they've had their
share of problems; it's perfect.
Avalon.
Works for me, says Hebe.
Tomorrow evening?
Stheno nods. I think we can
have Athena there then.
No sense drawing things out,

says Hebe. I'll see you there.
A gumdrop falls to the ground
and there is a rustle of wings,
and she is gone.

You really think Athena
will show up? asks Medusa,
half-excited, half-fearful.
I do, says Artemis, stepping up
to the trio. I will make sure of it.
If I must hunt her with my hounds,
if I must trap her with snares,
if I must carry her in a net,
she will be there.

Don't piss her off too much, says Medusa.

AVALON

How do ancient Greek immortals
travel to Avalon?
While the gorgons needed airfare
to get to Greece, and their own
feet and will to get to their cave,
and while Artemis's hounds needed
tokens and devices
to find their way to the underworld,
once in a mythological place,
goddesses
need no such things,
and Artemis moves herself and the gorgons
through places imagined
and real,
flickering
and liminal,
made of shadow
and stone.

They do, however, pack
hummus and pita bread,
olives and nuts,
warm socks and waterproof shoes,
and coats,
for the Isle may be damp

and cold.
Artemis breaks the news to Ladon
that he cannot accompany them.
But Hera and Io and Hecate can,
and walk with the gorgons from the cave to
the shore and, somehow, from that shore to
a distant shore, and onto a lush and green
and birdsong-spangled island.

It is colder, and a crisp wind plays with
Euryale's hair, long and curly, and Medusa
pulls her turban from a pocket to
cover her snakes and
keep them warm, and
Stheno's eyes drink in deep colors
of green and yellow and the sky is a
glaze of blue she has never seen before.
And here is a woman, welcoming them
and talking, and Stheno is still thirsty for
more blue, to be sated only when they are leaving.

Dark-skinned women mill about in a clearing
under trees that speak to the clouds
and whose leaves quilt a canopy.
Euryale embraces many of them:
I am so grateful for your generosity,
she says, your compassion.
Women stand together, says one Avalonian.
We may have a man sleeping on this island,

but this is a place of sisterhood. All are
safe here: you and your sisters, your goddesses—
she nods to Artemis, who is listening to
a group of priestesses—your ghosts—she nods again
and Euryale turns to find Hebe approaching,
carrying an urn. The urn is a deep red color,
chased with gold and silver and a line of
black paint so fine it is almost unseen.
Hebe is smiling and greeting the gathering
of women, and after a few moments,
she moves near the center of the clearing
with a small woman with silver braids.

The small woman with silver braids
enters the center of the clearing.
I am Vivian, she declares, opening her hands
and gesturing, and I
keep this land, which I offer for
peacemaking.

I bring Pallas, Hebe declares, holding the urn
gracefully in front of her heart and stepping
into the center of the clearing,
who has my protection and that of these
assembled.

Euryale and Stheno walk with Medusa
to the center of the clearing.
I am Medusa, she declares, removing her turban.

And I ask for the protection of
those assembled.

Artemis, flanked by Hecate and Hera,
steps into the center of the clearing.
I am Artemis, she says. I protect
Pallas, Medusa, and all those assembled.

Hera joins her. I am Hera,
she says, and I call Athena
to this assembly. I will stand for her,
and protect her if she desires.

There is a long moment of wind
and the scent of sharp cider apples
and water moving quickly and
then the sound of footsteps
in the wood, on the leaves
of past years.
An owl flies from a high branch
and lands on one above Vivian's
head, and the priestess smiles at it.
Old friend, she says, we want no harm.

And there she is: larger than the rest,
her body built up over centuries
with praise and uncritical citation,
in traditional armor
and flashing her grey eyes,

her mouth a thin line,
Athena.
She looks at Hera.
My father's wife summons me?
she asks.
I do, says Hera, but not alone:
and Hebe opens the urn.

PALLAS'S PLEA

The Avalon wind, unearthly,
spins up the ashes from Pallas's urn,
and out of the wind, the ashes
make a figure not unlike the one
Artemis saw in her dream.
Hebe stands proud and firm,
her feet planted
and arms embracing the urn
and then embracing
the ashy woman who
forms in front of overlarge Athena,
making the goddess of Athens
open her mouth
to gape and exhale:
Pallas?

The ash-woman turns her head,
gestures with her hands, steps forward
from Hebe's protective, encircling arms.
She opens her mouth, and the wind
runs through her body, shaking away
fragments of bone, but resonating in her
throat:

Athena

she says.
Her voice is soft and low and sorrowful.
You are martial in your appearance.
Would you kill me again?
I think am right to hide from you.
You have killed others, tortured
those
who loved you,
deceived gods and mortals alike,
your devotees the same as antagonists.

Athena's face is a maze of confusion:
lines run this way and that, her eyes
close in on one another, her lips jut forward,
her tongue licks them and her whole head shakes
silently no, no, and she is shrinking, her head growing smaller
and limbs drawing in towards her human-shaped body,
her plates of armor starting to fall against
each other like continents creating a
new world
and she stammers and Pallas
interrupts her ineffective vocalizations:

I am dead, and will not return to life
Pallas-of-ashes continues,
but I know how I died at your hand,
and though I am told

that your father conspired to end my life,
and you served as his tool,
I cannot be so sure,
for you have taken my name from me,
for your epithet, *warrior*, but do me
no honor in warring.

Athena's own face has begun to
gray, to ashen, in hearing Pallas's words.
Again she tries to speak, and again Pallas denies her,
and again she is diminished.

From my hiding place, says Pallas, I have had news
of others you have ended: for jealousy,
in rage, to amuse yourself.
First you feuded with my father's father,
and then damned his victim.
As *Athena Ergane*, you take credit
for art and craft, and yet drove Arachne
to suicide for excelling in your art.

Seeking fame and blood, you began a war,
and used my name there to glorify yourself,
and in patronizing heroes,
brought unhappiness to all you
would have served better by staying away.

And again Athena withers away, no longer
trying to defend herself.
She removes her helm
and rattles in her armor.

You show us none of your vaunted wisdom,
Pallas says, as ashes fly from her mouth:
you created slaves of the women of Troy
and madmen of those who battled for you—
in my name, unbestowed by me—
and took for yourself flight and winged
birds and their gleaming eyes.
You strike out before thinking—
as Tiresias knows well, and Marsyas,
and Ajax, and Diomedes' father, and
Erichthonius, and
so many unnamed women I could
weep a tear for each and never stop crying.

I am just! says Athena. I bring wisdom
to those who deserve it. I create heroes
and give them aid.
Her voice is strident.
Pallas's shakes, just a little:

Who deserves? she asks.
You are more jealous than Hera has ever been
and more fickle than your father with his lovers.
The owl flies away.

Medusa is crying and Hebe's face is solemn.
Athena gapes, still, at ash-Pallas, and
the Avalon wind grows colder, bringing rain
on its wings.

Athena, warrior, hero-protector,
unfathomable symbol of democracy,
lays down
her spear.
She begins to step forward,
but Vivian reaches out her hand
to keep the goddess in her place.
For the first time, Athena looks around
and finds that she is surrounded by
women she knows,
women with serious faces.

Pallas shakes her ashy head.
You are capricious, never-fast,
mutable.
Tell me you regret my death
and those of the women of Troy.
Tell me that you regret your
anger and torture of Medusa and
Arachne; of Aglaurus and Herse;
tell me that
your pride follows your heart now,
and not the other way around.
Tell me you embrace truth over

misplaced arrogance and impetuous
decisions.

Athena is incredulous.
She snatches up her spear,
pointing it at the circled women.
I have done what I must, she says,
and I do not regret becoming
myself: a great Olympian to be
worshipped, to be sought after,
to be lauded. I have won wars
and raised great men—

Euryale begins to interrupt,
but Vivian stays her. No,
Euryale says, respectfully, let me speak:

Yes, says Euryale, we know all about
your
"great men."
You have traded the lives of women—
hundreds, maybe more—
for your handful of
"great men."
Will you not consider the lives
of the women who loved you,
served you?

Artemis speaks:
Pallas, we seek to offer Athena a
new epithet, a new existence,
where she can be more thoughtful,
compassionate,
honest.
You have been as eloquent as
the dead can be, and I am grateful.
Medusa lowers her head to Pallas.
The rain comes harder, stinging,
and Pallas begins to dissolve.
Ashes weep down her face.
Why did you kill me? she asks Athena.
Why did you take my name from me?

Ash-Pallas begin to disperse.
Hebe makes a sweeping motion
with her right hand, and the ashes
still floating are returned to the urn.

Pallas, says Athena, *Pallas.*
She fears you, Hebe tells Athena.
You will not see her again,
not in any form, on any plane.

But I—Athena begins, and
her tongue and lips stop, because she
does not know where to go:
I wept for Pallas, she could say,

or I put up a little monument, but
men tore it down, or
you were my rival's descendent
and I should have killed you anyway
or
or that was so long ago I
don't really remember
what I did to you or
or I wish I was sorry, but
I'm not because I survived
and you didn't and I deserved
life more or
or
I didn't think you were really dead-dead
or
you just didn't matter that much to me.
And for the first time, Athena feels guilt and
grief and
her voice
refuses to work on her behalf.
But she swallows her pain
and her rage begins to grow again
and although she cannot speak her mind is afire
with loathing for these women who dare question her,
her, the foremost of goddesses.

Hera addresses Zeus's daughter.
When you were born, I rejoiced
as though you were my daughter also.

But I was jealous, as Pallas rightly said.
And I caused death, and violence,
and I was capricious and wrong. I made
women my enemy, but in truth I should
have been more angry at my husband and
his culture of use, and abuse.

You have lived that and come to believe
that your father could give your body away,
that your brother could war with you,
that you should compete with your sisters
to be held most beautiful, that beauty is
important.

Athena shakes her head, unable to speak
with rage choking her breath, no, but, I,
heroes—

Heroes, says Hecate, and Athena's head spins
to see the goddess, who holds a small torch
against the rain and drawing dark. Heroes, Athena?
My restless dead tell me of your heroes,
men who slaughtered them,
left on the roads to die. They ask me
for vengeance, not only against
Perseus and Bellerophon and Heracles,
but
you who armed those heroes,

encouraged them in their hunting,
deified them for hubris and brutality.

Athena inhales to prepare to speak.
Hecate, calm and with a gentle smile,
holds up her empty hand to stop her.

None of us can undo the past,
she says. I can no more bring back
sacrifices made to me and allow them
to live lives of happiness and fresh air
and car rides and squeaky toys than
my sister Selene can wake Endymion
or Apollo recall a farshot arrow.
And none of us, not even the gorgons,
seek your end, or your humiliation.
Her tone is light, she is optimistic that Athena
will agree:

We seek your brief absence, and
a new upbringing.

Athena stares at saffron-cloaked Hecate,
the torch burns low,
and a sliver of moon appears.

Athena, Hera says, come with me.
We will go to Lethe, and rest there until
our memories are faint and faded. We will take on

new human forms, and learn new worlds
and ways. I have done this; I remain myself,
but
a
sounder self,
a
self that has changed
and become
compassionate.

Athena is wrenched, her
immortal and cold heart
too large for her shrunken
ribcage,
banging chaotically
against her spine
and she feels a haughty reply
forming and yet
her bright eyes
are filled with liquid
harsher than the Styx
and as the rain falls through
the trees and into her
uncovered hair and
down her back,
she is angry and scared
and her fury boils up
and she shouts and spins on her heel
and the owl that had gone

returns a-wing and
flies at the goddesses
and gorgons,
clawing at their skulls
pulling away hair and flesh
and snakes come from
the Avalon soil and
wind tightly about their ankles
and as the gorgons
and goddesses
thrash,
arms and legs chaos before
Athena's armor and spear
and raising that spear to strike,
she screams at Medusa
how could you?
why aren't you ashamed?
and in it she says
how can you be alive?
how can you be famous?
celebrated?
why can't you die?
your life was mine
to judge and end!

and Medusa echoes back
in a whisper
how could you
and then her eyes harden

and she grabs a silver knife
from Vivian's belt
and slashes away a handful
of serpents and throws them
at Athena
and Athena writhes like the serpents
and then

Athena stops.

She stops.

Athena stops.

Athena
is stone.
The rain bounces from her shoulders,
runs across her face.
Medusa wheels to the sky,
arms wide and unmoored and
making vast circles with the knife,
its blade glinting under the
sliver of moon
and the owl vanishes
and the snakes slip away.

MUTABILITY

Duse, says Euryale,
softly, softly
but with a frightened edge to her voice.
Duse,
what did you do? How—
how did you do that?
She creeps towards her sister,
who spins gloriously
under the spinning sky.

Duse, says Euryale, motioning
for everyone else to stay back,
Duse,
breathe.

And spinning skylit Medusa
turns, and if remembering
her long-ago mortality,
takes a huge breath in,
and collapses to the ground,
the silver knife
a flash in the rain-wet grass.

Stheno steps in to her sister's side,
drops to the ground, holds her.
Duse, Duse, she says, like petting a cat.
Duse.

She raises her head, exhausted, and
looks at Stheno. I don't know, she says.
I don't know. She's immune—she can't—
I can't do that to her.
Euryale crouches with Stheno,
looking into her eyes. Stheno is calm,
but Euryale is scared.
Stroking her sister's back, Euryale looks up
at the assembled company.

Stheno stands and strides to Athena.
After a moment of hesitation,
she places her hand on the stone goddess's back
and leans in, listening.
She's alive, Stheno says. She pauses.
Perhaps because she is the source of Medusa's curse,
or because she is an immortal god, she is not dead.
She lives, but is...uncanny.

Duse, do you have any—
No, says Duse, still crying, her face red
and angry. I didn't even
look at her.

You'd know—everyone else here would be stone
as well. I didn't even think this could happen—
I just—
just
just wanted to make a gesture,
to make you all safe,
to protect you all,
the serpents.
Even now the shorn spots on her head
are filling with new snakes, small and soft,
harmless, blind babies.

Vivian swoops forward to the ground, a hawk:
her hand strikes out and recoils,
ready to parry;
she lifts her dagger
and a tiny serpent,
holds it close and light,
listening, smelling.
She turns to Medusa,
sheathing her dagger.
You have more power, she says to Medusa,
than you may ever know.
Your impulse—
to protect
to avenge
to heal

others—
has given you
might.

Hebe, who holds the urn of Pallas's
spectral ashes still in her arms,
considers this new truth.
We are mutable creations,
says the goddess of youth:
the gorgons show us that.

What I did, says Medusa, rising to
a kneeling position, was emotional,
a plea for recognition, a, a, an outburst;
I wanted her to look at me and see
the damage she has done.

She looks frantically to each of the goddesses
seeking anger and
finding none.
Am I wrong to have wanted such change in her?
I have altered her,
controlled her body
without her consent.
How am I any better than she?

You protected us, says Stheno.

Hebe speaks softly. I was so afraid,
she says. You protected me,
you protected all
of us.

There is a collective,
if still shaky,
sigh
rushing from the clearing
to seas far away.

Vivian dismisses the priestesses
and smiles at Hera. Time to go, I think,
says Hera. This could have been so much worse
in our own world, she says; thank you, Vivian.
Vivian nods, and clasps each woman in turn.
To Stheno, she whispers: what is healing
will heal, and ten steps later, the gorgons
and goddesses find themselves back in
the gorgons' seaside cave, a large stone
in tow.

What did she say to you? asks Euryale of Stheno.
She said that healing heals, or something like that.
Ten steps is not far, but Avalon is far from Greece,
and all journeys are tiring.
I need to sleep on it, says Stheno.
Can we put that—her—somewhere out of sight?
she asks, nodding to the stone.

Euryale nods, and a group of nymphs
immediately surround her.

We are mutable, Medusa thinks as she
falls unconscious. Mutable.
What is healing heals. Stheno's mind
rolls about the phrase, what is healing,
heals, will heal, what is healing,
healing will heal,
what is healing?
Euryale slumps down with
the nymphs, who hold her
all night long.
And Artemis and Hecate
encircle the cave with protection
charms, blessing everyone as
they sleep.

The sea splashes onto the beach.
Ladon turns in his sleep, sending salt air into
the cave.

SALT

Salt water, says Medusa, before the moon has set.
Salt water, says Stheno, before she moves her eyelids.
Salt water, says Euryale, before kissing a beautiful nymph.

It might remove the stone casing.
It might heal her wounds.
It might soothe her irritations.

If it doesn't? asks Hecate.
We'll figure something out, says Euryale.
We'll leave her as stone, says Stheno.
I'll put her in my garden, says Medusa, her eyes still puffy and red,
but her mind sharp and tart,
and decorate her for the seasons, like a giant stone goose.
She gets side-eyes. What, she says, it's an American thing.
And if she can still torment me from
inside that sarcophagus, well,
we'll figure something out.

A plynteria, then, says Hecate, a little too brightly.
Oh, says Stheno, I hadn't thought of that.
I was thinking of the Styx, to wash away hatred,
or the Lethe, to wash away memory,
or Acheron, to wash away pain.
We'd have to drag this to the Underworld?

asks Euryale, I vote no, even if we could get in.
Do the rivers even do that? asks a nymph.
Not mine, says the nymph Styx, who has
been there the whole time listening to
Acadian folk music with a small Cerberean puppy
in her lap.
Hera turns to her. Lethe can do that, she says.
Yes, says Styx patiently, but I can't.
What I can do is help bless a plynteria.

I don't know about the rest of you,
says Aegle, cooking eggs over a flame,
but that sounds like a mortal thing,
and since I live on an enchanted island
with a dragon—Ladon looks up and is
rewarded with a piece of toast—
I don't know what that is or what it does
or why you think it'll put the rock god over there
in a better mood.

Oh, oh, pick me, pick me, says a Nereid,
laughing lazily. She sits up straighter:
I remember those.
She becomes more solemn, her eyes enlarging
and her voice deepening.
People would close the temples of Athena,
wrapping them with cords
to prevent any from entering;
undress their statues of her,

cover the statues in a special cloth,
carry them to springs or sea,
and wash them;
all the while
ritual fires devoured
the old garments,
uneaten food in the temple,
papers past use.
It was a dangerous day:
no business was transacted
less the absence of the goddess
taint it.

She pauses, and continues,
more lightly,
people also ate lots of figs.
I never got that part.
But to perform it—
the plynteria—
you need a genos of
praxiergidai—women sharing
a name, a common bloodline.
Everyone here has that, basically—

We should do it, says Stheno.
We are the genos needed for this
bathing of the goddess.
She is earnest, almost embarrassingly so
to her sisters: We are healers,

we are from her rival's territory,
we ask for her hatred and
scorn to be washed away,
we know how to use the
healing and magical properties
of salt water—the other sea gods can help,
and those of the land or air can
burn old garments
and make new ones.

Stheno's cheeks redden as her
words are met
with silence.
We have to try, at least.
It's not quite a question.

It could be even better than
submitting to Lethe, says Hera.
I don't know, says Euryale:
taking a bath has never done much for
me when I'm angry.
It's a ritual bath, says Medusa,
and we can burn all of her stuff
that reeks of bad juju.
I cannot believe you said that word,
says Stheno. Juju? You?
Aren't we interfering with her,
without her consent? says Euryale.
I'm not sure about this.

Her own worshippers used to do it,
says the Nereid, it was a major festival.
So there's precedent,
and it's an established practice that
is supposed to honor her, not degrade her.
True, says Hera.
It's not like we're sending her home
from school because she has lice.
They all look at her.
What? she says. I'm a mother.
She continues: this is a worshipful practice,
and we need to find a way to un-stone her.
I don't want to break her with a hammer—
Medusa starts to raise her hand to volunteer and Hera
gives her a look—so let's try this. If nothing else,
we are trying to heal her from her own anger, and Medusa's.

PREPARATIONS

They are all very, very careful.

Hecate and Stheno create a protective space,
whispering together over olive pits
and oil
and herbs
and seaweed.

Euryale and Medusa ask Aphrodite and Artemis
for blessings of peace; asking outright for success
seems hubristic.
The goddesses do, although neither
feels certain that this is a good idea.
I mean, what if she emerges and
calls her dad and he burns us all? asks
Aphrodite. I have things to do.

Hebe arrives.
I brought the figs, she says with jollity.
Medusa thins her lips at Hebe, but
Euryale takes the gift as it is,
and covers them
with honey.
Hebe lingers with Medusa.
Medusa rubs her fingers over the

newly growing snakes.
Athena will never understand what
Pallas and I have suffered,
even if we get her to leave me alone.
She uses an older serpent's teeth
to prick open her finger,
Euryale's earlobe,
and Stheno's lower lip.

The Hesperides crush fennel
and purslane
and mix them
with fingertips dipped in
vinegar.

To these they add:
clay from Thebes;
filings from an Athenian coin;
ancient rainwater from Thessaly;
salt and rock from the cave's
sea entrance;
three dried-up seahorses;
a single olive;
pumice;
a page from a mythology book,
torn into long strands and
caramelized,
then tossed with
salt and sumac;

sheep fat;
cattle flesh;
gorgon blood
(a tiny drop from each,
mingled together on
Hecate's adularescent
fingernail);
ground almonds;
an eyelash from
Hélène Cixous;
snail mucin;
and tears from the
slaves from Troy,
saved for many years.
This makes the
cleaning paste
for the ritual.

(The Hesperides
are making it up
as they go along,
trusting history,
myth,
intuition.)

The Nereids weave a long purple cloth
as they stand in the seawater,
the sun playing on their scales
and fingernails.

Athena may have done wrong,
but this ceremony must still
give her honor,
save her face.

Would you be bored,
Euryale asks Aphrodite,
without humans, rubbing her
earlobe with a finger.
Or those of us
who pass for them?
Is it all just entertaining drama
for the gods?

Aphrodite takes Euryale's hand
and sucks on her finger,
looking serious and seductive.
Then she giggles and kisses Euryale
on the cheek.
No! she says. Well, maybe for some.
I just like making people happy.
Ares doesn't care about the people
he sends to war—it feeds his rage;
Athena honestly thinks she does good things
for humanity by being the patron of heroes.
The gods have reasons. It's not like we
sit around on clouds watching an ant farm.

The cave cools and warms again and cools
once more. The moon and sun
rise and fall and dance a tango
with the stars and the tide visits
and leaves and returns again.
Ladon is petted, Artemis's hounds
play on the edge of the sea,
Medusa's snakes stretch and recoil.
In the morning, Athena will be bathed.
For this night, though, she rests in a niche
of her own, lit with oil lamps and
hung with sea-made ornaments and figs,
slowly drying in the air.

PLYNTERIA

Let us begin a wonder tale.

Let us begin a new myth, the story of Athena Plynteria.

Athena, raised by men to be a warrior, has served her warlike purpose
overlong. She champions heroes, warrior men who sacrifice living animals
to her and who conquer—and all that conquering entails, pillage and
slavery and killing and yes, rape—in her name. She feuds with men and
women alike, over territory and beauty, but so great is her dedication to the
men of her culture and her demands of an uncertainly defined chastity of
her acolytes that when even her greatest rival rapes her priestess, Athena is
angrier at the woman than the god. Clearly, her devotee led him on, said
something suggestive, had too much to drink, wore something provocative.

A slight young woman
wears jeans,
a sweatshirt,
and boots.
She has short hair
and wears no makeup.
This
is what I was wearing,
her sign says.
Tell me I was asking for it.
When Hephaestus attacked Athena, she fought him off. Surely, her sworn
women could do the same of men attacking them, regardless if the men in
question are gods.

No Means No,
says the sign
a woman holds up.
Next to her, a man
carries
a sign reading
End Victim Blaming.

Time has changed the world,
but not Athena.
But now, despite
the gorgons' calls
for peaceful negotiation,
Athena's rage
frozen by Medusa's protection
has ended Athena's
activity.

In her stone state,
she cannot fight anyone,
or give succor to warriors
who fight
and rape
in her name.
In the heat of the moment,
perhaps Medusa meant
only to stop Athena's
harassment;

perhaps she wanted
revenge;
perhaps she wanted
the god to experience
helplessness.

Athena now
is the woman in the trap,
pinned down,
immobilized,
without agency,
silenced,
forced into
something
she doesn't want.
She is now every woman
who has been grabbed,
choked, weighed down,
pushed, battered,
held by the hair,
bruised, kicked,
violated.

And she must now rely
on compassion,
given freely to her,
a gift she has never given.

The Hesperides drape Athena
with the cloth,
and the gorgons
and their sisters
carry her out of the cave
down to the sea.

Stheno has lost track
of time:
the month, the season;
there is just today.
But a stormwind
is coming to them,
sending tastenotes
of cinnamon and chocolate
on its sharp forward edge.
It is the scent of autumn
to her.

The purple drape around Athena
swings in the wind,
something beyond a flutter,
but not quite a billow.
Wearing only clean skin
anointed with oil,
her bearers step into the water.
Like coffin-carriers, they
slowly remove the stone
from their shoulders.

Enyo wears the eye and
guides her Graeae sisters.

The stone rests in the cool water,
Athena's legs and side just covered by
the sweet salty foam.
Further, says Medusa,
and with caressing hands, they
move her lower until only
her head and torso remain
in the air.

Medusa leads.
She takes the Hesperides' scrub
and, settling herself fully
beneath the water,
kneeling like the supplicant
she once was,
begins to wash the goddess.

She is gentle and slow,
like her sisters were
following her rape.
Around her, her sisters
balance the stone god
in the water.
Around them,
goddesses and nymphs,
Ladon and hounds

encircle the
gorgons and Phorcides,
sending away fish that would nibble.
An enormous ray makes a pass,
but only to tell the women that
Poseidon is being entertained
by Phorcys and Ceto in an
exceptional, days-long diversion.
Euryale smiles: they may not be seen
often, she says, but they are never
not our parents.

Medusa begins with the toes,
scooping scrub into one hand,
dipping her fingers into it,
and applying it to Athena's
hard, grey digits. She anticipates
the feel of flesh as she works
but
there is nothing
there is only water beneath the stone
and Medusa
turns her head and
jerks it,
motion that makes Stheno
come to her immediately.

Duse?

She's not here,
says Medusa.
She is very calm,
stating a fact,
but her words are clipped,
and Stheno can hear Medusa's
back teeth grate on one another.

Stheno's chest feels as if
iron bands surround it, and
she kneels with her sister,
taking up scrub and Athena's calf.
Artemis, from the forward circle,
looks back at her devotee
with concern, and Stheno
replies by widening her eyes
at her patron.

Athena's calf is muscled and thick
and Stheno washes it with heavier
hands and ritual scrub than Medusa
applied to her toes, and
as she
works her hands
over the goddess's leg
it

falls away
to

nothing.

Medusa stands:
sisters, she says,
her voice beginning to shake
and Stheno's hand
on her arm doing little
to stabilize her,
sisters.

The Graeae and outer guard
all turn and Euryale
begins, frantically,
to tear at Athena's stone
back and the goddess
begins to break in the
salt water
and all three gorgons
not quite panicked but
very
close
grab handfuls of the
sweet-smelling
magenta-colored
body polish,
scouring the hands,

the breasts, the thighs
and the stone
continues to break
open
and hollow
and full of no flesh,
no goddess,
but air

and as it cracks
with thousands of
fault lines
and broken veins,
the head begins to
topple in to the water
and as Medusa catches it
in her hands,
bright as blood
with purifying luster,
the forehead cracks
and the two halves of
the head dissolve into sand
and in her hands

is a
baby.

A small baby.
A wet baby.

A girl baby.
A fingers-strong-as-iron baby.
A yelling baby.

From the head of Athena
has sprung
a baby girl.
It is, mythologically speaking,
a reversal.
A mirror, a retcon,
a re-write, a parody, a
counterfeit,
a burlesque, an echo—
no. A new incarnation,
a new manifestation,
a new Athena.

Euryale takes the baby
from a stunned Medusa
while Stheno strides
through thigh-deep water,
churning it with the miniscule
granular remains of stone Athena
and up onto the shore and into
the cave.

BIRTH MAGIC

Moirai! Stheno calls, her voice
a mixture of command,
pleasure, and chagrin.
The Fates had not left
the cool, quiet cave
to witness the plynteria,
staying behind to work
and drink with Lethe and Styx.

Ladies, Stheno says as she approaches them.

Ooh, says Clotho in a
stage whisper to her sisters,
it worked! it worked!
Lachesis sighs happily.
Can we help you? asks Atropos, pert.

Stheno opens her mouth,
tilts her head,
closes it again. She taps her fingers
along her hip.

There is a silent standoff.
It's not hostile; in fact
everyone seems to be trying

very hard to keep
from exploding into
laughter, the laughter of
relief and of absurdity and of
glee.

Atropos finally clears her throat
and speaks:
Her daimon, Athena's,
she explains,
had become so very small.
She could not inspire heroes;
she could not function as a god.

Gods change, you see, she said.
As we do. They must, or
people can no longer believe in them
or what they stood for.
If they cannot change and
show compassion for the
people who love them and the
times in which those people live,
they shrink, and disappear.

You thought perhaps Athena
had grown in power because of
new worshippers,
giving her strength.
There was a little of that,

but it was mostly anger,
anger she recycled to use
against Medusa.

I think perhaps too… says Clotho,
her hands never stopping,
always spinning and thinning
a cloudy fleece-like stuff
with her beautiful fingers,
twisting and twining.
I think perhaps, too,
Athena knew her wrongs
against mortals, but as Medusa
rightly discerned,
she was too proud
to admit them.

We allot lives,
says Lachesis,
and we can entangle them,
weaken them,
reinforce them.
Athena's thread, once robust,
was infinitely fine, but knotted
in difficult ways
and put her portion
into disrepair.

Only when Medusa
cast down her serpents—
an act born out of fear
and unthinkable sadness
and compassion and love and protection—
did Athena's thread
begin to rub
along my shears.
Atropos's words are like a song.

We called on a friend,
Eileithyia,
to help us,
she continues.
Eileithyia! chimes in Clotho,
she was there when this all began,
when Athena sprung like
a gazelle, long-limbed,
with sharp eyes,
from the head of Zeus.

And so did I attend once again,
says Eileithyia, who seems to appear
from nowhere, but is really just stepping
in from a deeper part of the cave,
where she has been napping after
working much magic on Athena's thread
and contributing, secretly, to the
Hesperides' ritual bath scrub.

Your cave is lovely, she tells Stheno;
I live in one too of course, but
mine has stalactites that rather get
in the way of entertaining large groups.
They are good for laboring mothers
to hold onto, though.

Stheno, who had no idea at all that
this daughter of Hera had come to
the party,
bows to stall to find words,
and then says,
you and yours are always welcome here;
it has often been a place of endings,
but is also a place of beginnings
and re-birth, if not exactly birth.

Eileithyia squeezes Stheno's hands
in gratitude, and then sits near Lachesis,
where she peers over the Fate's shoulder
at the strands in her lap.

Her thread was a mess, says Eileithyia:
knotted and fraying and twisted backwards.
It was easy to see where she had gone wrong,
hurt those she should have helped,
and vice versa.
Inside her stone sarcophagus,
Athena dwindled:

she was aghast that Medusa's power could work against her,
but the fact that it did proved to her
that she was not surviving the modern world
well at all.
Her thread was rotting,
and there was so little attached to it
of her own essence that we all together
made a determination:
parts of her self would need
to be pared away
if she was to live.
Clotho plucked aside dead, anger-whitened
strands, and restored those that will
grow into wisdom
and justice;
Lachesis measured a new infinite span,
as only she can do;
Atropos cut the strands Clotho removed;
and I refashioned Athena's daimon
into a baby.

Together with Hera,
who once sought
to keep me away from a birth,
and my sister Artemis,
and my sister Hebe
(who brought delicious figs),
and my sister Nemesis
we invoked our greatest powers,

and together we sang
and spun
a new infant Athena
into life.

And about that baby,
Stheno begins.
She'll be fostered,
says Hera, who has
stepped in and is drying
her short curly hair
with a green beach towel.
Actually, in this day and age,
she'll be formally adopted.
I have the perfect family
for her.
She shakes her head
and runs her fingers through
her hair and it bounces
happily, like Medusa's snakes.
Mutability, Stheno thinks.

Euryale and Duse enter the cave,
Euryale still carrying Athena.
She crosses to the Fates and
Eileithyia: here she is,
your little wonder,

flesh and daimon together.
The baby yawns and stretches,
and each Fate kisses her forehead.

Eileithyia draws a little circle
just above the baby's dark eyebrows:
grow and be whole,
and when you are grown
and whole,
know us once more,
and come to us,
for we love you.

Worship plain
and powerless
Eleos,
compassion,
and be taught by time
that your heart
should glow
for others,
and melt,
thaw,
and resolve
their pain.

Mutability.

AFTERPARTY

Hera and Io depart first,
wrapping baby Athena in
the purple fabric once meant
as a shroud,
now proving a swaddle.

Ladon eats almost everything,
so there's little need to clean up.
The Hesperides drag him away,
laughing and happy,
demanding promises of visits
and email.

Guests depart slowly,
a train leaving the station
in grand style.

Nymphs come and go,
dallying with Euryale
and sometimes Duse,
and finally wave goodbye
blowing kisses.

Stheno sleeps through
much of the leave-taking.

She has started to miss her bed
at home, and *gati*, and
sugarcane soda.
Exhausted, she sleeps
deeply, but her dreams
are full of rest:
she often dreams of
night skies
over vast soft fields,
breezes that carry woodsmoke
instead of salt,
apples sweet in color
and flavor
and scent.

Medusa submits to the
nymphs and dryads,
making terrible jokes about wood
and lolling about in
post-orgasmic splendor
for several days.
And then one morning,
she wakes early
and goes out to the sea.

She floats and then
sinks
to the
bottom,

watching fish
and listening
to her heart,
which beats
even when it
doesn't need to.
Is she safe, now,
after magic and betrayal
and metaphors made material?
Will her sleep be safe,
outside of the cave,
in America,
in the mundane world?

Her curse will never be lifted:
she has always known that.
Athena was known to strike out,
do something terrible and fixed,
reconsider just a bit, and ameliorate
part of her punishments; she
could never reverse them.
Medusa's serpents bob
with the underwater currents,
serene and weightless,
sensing the slenderest
rays of sun that reach them
in the depths.

The surrounding whisper
of water reassures her:
she will sleep
without Athena's dreams,
without bulls and swords
and shields and gods.
She will sleep
and dream of the sea,
calm and quiet,
her cradle rocking.

AUTUMN

In Paris, there is a soft
autumn rain
and leaves on the cobbled streets
and under a cozy duvet,
Euryale is curled up
next to a lover,
dreaming of their upcoming
vacation to the countryside.

In New England,
Medusa is on
campus escort duty,
walking students to
and from parties
and haunted houses
and laughing with them
about books and costumes
and pumpkin spice everything
and her serpents,
happy and warm,
are nestled close to her scalp,
satin on silk,
and she is
content.
It's a perfect night for

trick-or-treating, and
Stheno is sitting on the
front porch of her
house.

She's petting a cat and rummaging
through the bowl of candy for her
favorites (Three Musketeers, because
everything comes in threes),
so she's not fully paying attention
when the girl in the long pink dress
comes up and says the magic words.
Before Stheno takes in the full costume,
she asks what are you?
because if nothing else the girl's
dress looks vaguely Jane Austen-ish,
but as the last word leaves her mouth
she sees the plush owl
strapped to the girl's head with
a long cord that ties under
her chin
and the girl says,
excitedly,
Athena!
From Greek mythology?
But a nice version,
she goes on,
one who would have
sent Odysseus home right away,

and not been mad at Arachne,
and, you know, all that.

So you are,
says Stheno,
amazement turning into
delight
in the crisp wind,
noticing the girl's
moms waiting at the curb
with other children,
so you are.
You get extra candy.
Keep an eye out for
those little kids
with you tonight,
she says
and the girl nods, solemnly,
and goes off
with the group,
her arm
around a smaller
child,
the plastic shield
on her back
banging with every step:
a forward march.

ABOUT THE AUTHOR

Kendra Preston Leonard is a poet, lyricist, and librettist whose work is inspired by the local, historical, and mythopoeic. She is especially interested in addressing issues of social justice, the environment, and disability through poetry. Her first chapbook, *Making Mythology*, was published in 2020 by Louisiana Literature Press, and her work appears in numerous publications including *vox poetica*, *lunch*, *These Fragile Lilacs*, and *Upstart: Out of Sequence: The Sonnets Remixed*. Leonard collaborates regularly with composers on works for voice including new operas and song cycles. Her lyrics and libretti have been set by composers including Jessica Rudman, Rosśa Crean, and Allyssa Jones. The author of numerous scholarly books and articles, Leonard is also a musicologist and music theorist, and her academic work focuses on women and music in the twentieth and twenty-first centuries; music and the early modern; and music and screen history.

Follow her on Twitter (@K_Leonard_PhD) or visit her site at https://kendraprestonleonard.hcommons.org/.

About the Press

Unsolicited Press was established in 2012 and is based in Portland, Oregon. The team produces poetry, fiction, and nonfiction by award-winning and emerging writers.

Learn more at www.unsolicitedpress.com.

CPSIA information can be obtained
at www.ICGtesting.com
Printed in the USA
BVHW081411120122
625992BV00009B/287

9 781950 730636